girl, at my window

V.F. Gingerelli

ISBN: 979-8-2841-9426-3
Printed in the United States of America
First Edition
Copyright © 2025 by V.F. Gingerelli
All rights reserved.

No part of this publication may be reproduced, distributed, or transmitted in any form or by any means, including photocopying, recording, or other electronic or mechanical methods, without the prior written permission of the publisher, except in the case of brief quotations embodied in critical reviews and certain other noncommercial uses permitted by copyright law.

This is a work of fiction. Names, characters, places, and incidents either are the product of the author's imagination or are used fictitiously. Any resemblance to actual persons, living or dead, events, or locales is entirely coincidental.

Girl, at My Window
by V.F. Gingerelli

Forward

You are not defined solely by your past, nor are you confined to the version of yourself others may perceive. You are not just what you have done—you are what you will do, what you will see, and who you will become.

Today, like every new day, is a chance for renewal, hope, and growth. No matter your history, you are full of potential. You have the power to do better, to be better, and to live more joyfully—for yourself and those around you.

You will never stop growing. There is always more to see, more to love, and countless small wonders to appreciate, no matter how insignificant they may seem. Pay attention.

Everything will be okay. The sun will rise tomorrow, and you will keep moving forward.

This page is intentionally left blank.

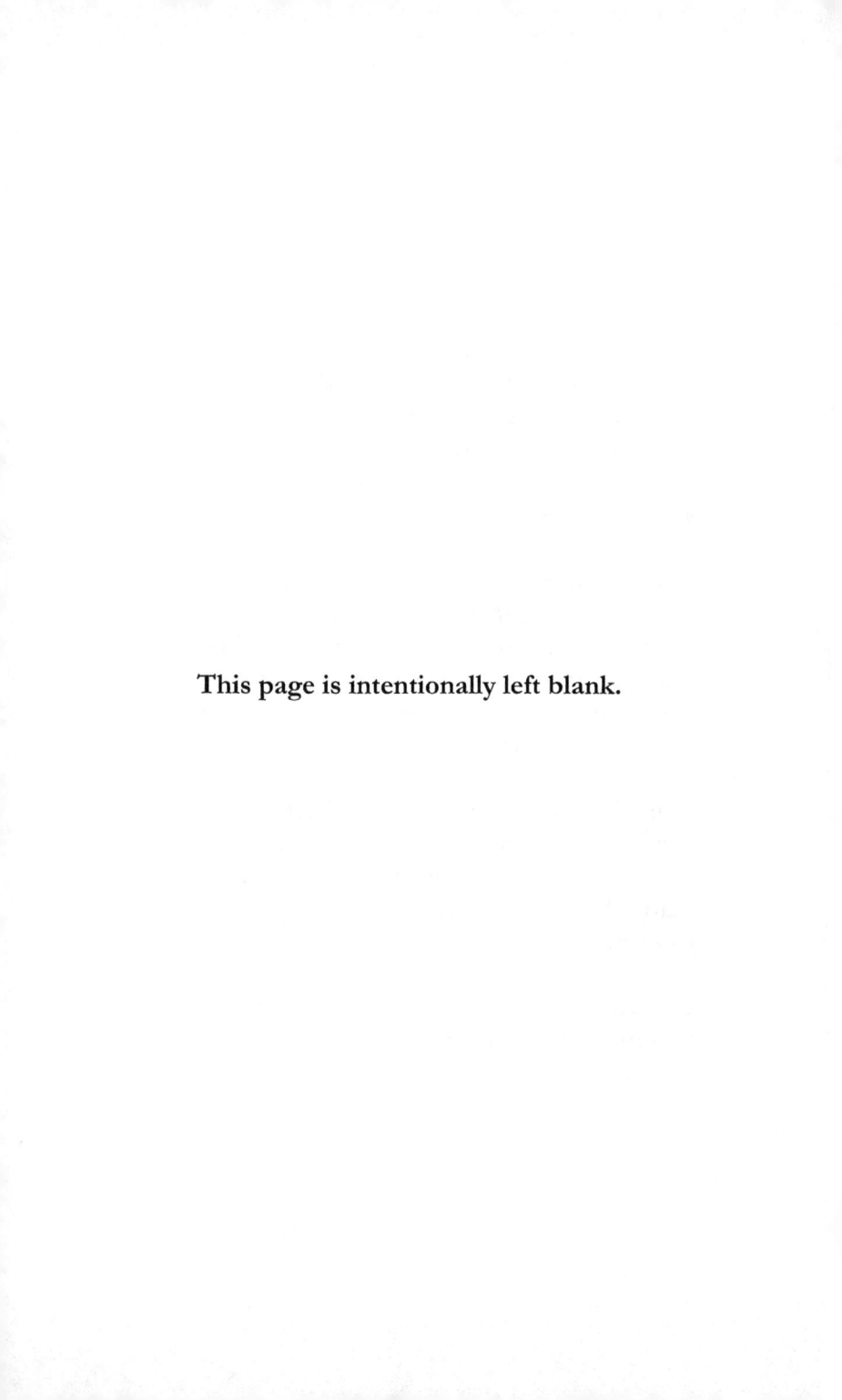

V.F. Gingerelli

Emma

She...wasn't "normal," she wasn't like the other kids, and didn't have regular things or regular activities. No one was wondering what she was doing or, if her friends were being nice at school. In that place, during the time that passed, She just existed.

    A cold mist drew over the small pond behind Emma's house, it was morning and spring had officially arrived. The flowers and trees began to bloom and bud with the hope of growth and new life. For most, spring is a welcomed change. It arrived in contrast to the cold distant winter, the short days and long nights which typically prohibited activities that warmer weather allows.

Girl, at My Window

She, did not know any of this, she did not know of this change, she never felt the joy that the spring renewal brought us, the gift in the changing seasons.

Her existence was static, cold, routine. When the light of the day went away, the cold enveloped her, and she felt an emptiness that despite all attempts would not subside. The mind of a child, like Emma, is a creative and beautiful world, impossibly possible. Tragically not all feel the escape and the wonder that accompanies that dream like state.

She did not experience the opportunity to believe in anything more than here and now. It was not where she was going or what would she do for her life just …. was. No mystery, no plans.

The girl was nearly the same age as Emma. They even looked as if they could be sisters in a different life. So close, yet so far, had never been a more resounding cliché for these two girls. Their experiences, their perspectives, their futures looked so vastly different. In fact, it is possible that until now, they had never had a similar thought inside their heads.

For her this was not a life of flowers and fun, one protected by caring parents and family. For her, this was a completely different world, one that even the most creative person would not dream of for a child.

      Emma lived in a quiet neighborhood that seemed to hum with peace. The newly built homes boasted freshly turned mulch beds with a robust assortment of shrubbery, well-manicured lawns and flower beds brimming with color. Red and grey bricks lined those same flower beds against their freshly cut green lawns. Birds chirped from the branches of old oak trees that lined the forest on the back of each property, their leaves rustling gently in the breeze. It was the kind of neighborhood that made you think of perfect summer days, where the sun never set too early, and the air was always warm and inviting. A place where the same white mailboxes, freshly paved driveways and tree lined roads indicated a uniform peace among the homes in the neighborhood.

      The type of neighborhood where if you didn't pay attention well enough, you may go on, day after day, not noticing any difference at all.

      At six years old, Emma found joy in the little things—the same way many children do. The way the sunlight danced on the surface of the pond in the park, the feel of the cool grass under her bare feet, and the smell of fresh rain that often followed an afternoon thunderstorm. She was a curious little girl, always asking questions, her bright eyes wide with wonder as she explored her world.

Girl, at My Window

Emma would stop to examine every ant marching across the sidewalk, every butterfly that fluttered past her, and even the tiniest of rocks that caught her attention, as if they held secrets she was meant to uncover.

Although unaware, She was not so lucky. She never felt the sun's rays warming her skin or, the joy of a sweet treat from a loving parent. Her only friend was a small muddied up doll that often sat in the corner, only listening to the same old mumblings, over and over again. Day after day the doll heard the same, rehearsed speech, clawing her way through the daily routine, begging for some interaction, a sliver of normal life outside this place.

Otherwise, she had nothing to call her own. None of what she did or who she was really mattered. Even if it did, she couldn't know any different. She had nothing to miss, no experience to yearn for. In the mind of this child, her world just the way it was, and as well as she was aware, that was good enough for her.

Emma's father, Bryan, was the kind of man who was always sweet and patient. Mom and dad loved each other, and Emma knew their hugs, kisses and late-night kitchen dancing sessions proved that. Bryan worked as an architect, and though his job kept him busy, he always made time for Emma. He would kneel to her level, listening intently as she talked about her day or told him about her latest discoveries. Once a week they would break out their crayons, markers and paint and, with the utmost precision, they would draw out intricate architectural designs, led of course by the imagination of a 6-year-old, future architect. When they were done, as promised, dad would carry them to work for inspiration. Bryan loved the way Emma's mind worked, he trusted her, she was his pride and joy. She was so bright, always asking questions that made him pause and think. She reminded him of himself when he was younger, always searching for answers and seeing the world through a lens of curiosity.

Emma's mother, Lynn, was gentle and nurturing, with a warmth that could fill up a room. She worked as a schoolteacher and had a natural gift for making everyone feel comfortable and valued. In Bryan's eyes, Lynn was a near superhero figure; her empathy and determination to do better, be better, and make everyone around her happier was an almost mythical trait. A full-time mom, best friend, and wife who never ever stopped loving or creating new and exciting memories.

Emma held a very special place in Lynn's heart. Emma was their miracle child, their long-awaited perfect

Girl, at My Window

masterpiece. Emma was the result of two people giving every ounce of love they had, to each other, every day. Byran and Lynn were lucky, they now were able to share that same love with Emma.

While Bryan was the one who often led the conversations with Emma about the world, it was Lynn who helped her find the beauty in the everyday moments. She would sit with Emma, drawing pictures together, teaching her the names of flowers, or reading books that opened Emma's imagination to the farthest corners of the universe.

Despite the love, support and adventures supplied by her parents, Emma was a shy little girl. Her inquisitive nature led her to learn and observe that the world was a big place, full of wonder and amazement. Still, many of those questions born from the mind of a 6-year-old remained unanswered. At school, she kept to herself, observing from the sidelines rather than jumping into the hustle and bustle of the other kids. Her classmates often seemed to be in a hurry, running around, shouting to one another, or playing games with an energy that Emma found both exhilarating and overwhelming. She wasn't scared of the other children, but the idea of joining in felt like stepping into an unknown world, one that she wasn't sure how to navigate.

V.F. Gingerelli

She was shy too; she was afraid of most everything outside of that place, she certainly would have been on the sidelines, watching, quietly overwhelmed. She had never known a life outside of this, outside of this dark and cold place.

Winter had just ended and finally some comfort was felt in the warmth which, inch by inch, seemed to warm the fridged dirt beneath her feet. It was the only thing she had to look forward to, the only difference in her reality, was the changing of the seasons. In between the cold and hot were her favorite of course, just the right feeling, just enough so that the precious water they had didn't freeze, or their skin didn't boil. Finally, some level of comfort had come as spring arrived.

Emma preferred the quiet moments with her parents, the slow pace of the evenings when they would sit on the porch and watch the sunset together, or when they would read stories before bed. She wasn't lonely—but imagined a life like the other kids, those kids whose brothers and sisters antagonized them at playtime but when the day was settled would cuddle up with them at night. Someone to share your favorite snack with or imagine you are in a spaceship together, off to a faraway planet.

Girl, at My Window

When Emma wasn't exploring the world outside, she was often in her room, surrounded by her favorite books and toys. She would make up elaborate stories, with kingdoms and dragons, princesses and pirates, or talk to the animals that lived in her backyard, believing they could understand her.

Still, there were moments when Emma felt a longing to be part of the world that seemed so vibrant and full of life around her. She wanted to be as confident as the other kids, to play without hesitation, to speak without the worry that her words might be wrong. Sometimes, as she watched the other children laughing and running, she would imagine simply joining them, throw caution to the wind, and let herself be swept up in the joy they seemed to share so easily. Emma was happy- and still there was something that wasn't quite right. Something different, something strange, a missing piece.

She knew none of this, she couldn't choose to be happy or unhappy, as if no feeling at all was a way to cope. To numb the life that she wasn't living. She had no toys, no happiness and no knowledge that something was amiss. Her life revolved around a few square feet and despite this reality, and unbeknownst to her, a dangerous opportunity lie ahead that could completely reimagine her world.

V.F. Gingerelli

She

One morning, after breakfast, Emma sat at the kitchen table, her small fingers tracing the edge of the cereal bowl as she stared out the window. The sun was shining, the sky was blue, and it looked like another perfect day. Her mother, Lynn, was busy packing her bag for work, and her father, Bryan, was reading the newspaper, though he had one eye on Emma, sensing her quiet mood.

"Emma," Lynn said gently, turning to her daughter with a soft smile.

"What do you think about going to the park today? You haven't been there in a while. Maybe we can have a picnic."

Girl, at My Window

Emma looked up, her brow furrowing slightly as she considered the idea. She loved the park, but there were always so many other children there, running and playing, and Emma often felt like an outsider in their world. Still, she didn't want to disappoint her mother.

"I... I guess that sounds nice," she said softly, her voice almost a whisper.

Bryan, who had been listening, set the newspaper aside and leaned toward Emma.

"Hey, you know, there's no rush. We'll take it slow, okay? If you feel like you just want to sit and watch the ducks for a while, that's perfectly fine."

Emma smiled, feeling comforted by her father's words. She loved when he spoke to her like that, giving her the space to be herself without pressure. She knew he understood her in a way that no one else could.

She understood none of that. She experienced none of that.

She did not know the safety of a porch swing, nor the gentle cadence of her father's voice reading bedtime stories.

V.F. Gingerelli

She had never watched the sun melt into the horizon with the promise of tomorrow. No one had ever placed toys in her hands or taught her the names of animals or wrapped her in warm blankets and whispered that she was loved.

For as long as she could remember, this was her life. This place. A small dim existence. Only a shadow of light leaking in from a crack in the roof above. The air was stagnant, sour with mildew and rot, and filled with the scent of damp earth and fear.

Her world was defined by absence.

No joy. No pain. No understanding. Just a kind of vast nothingness that coiled around her like fog, soft and suffocating. And perhaps worse than fear was the lack of anything to fear. She could not even conjure a name for her emptiness. She was not lonely because she did not know companionship. She was not sad because she had never tasted happiness. Feeling nothing had become her way of surviving the life that she had never truly lived.

This world was smaller than any world that could possibly fit the imagination of even the dullest child. But she did not have the imagination of a child, more of an animal and, by design, that is how she was meant to feel.

Girl, at My Window

Her home was dark and crowed. Even when the sun was high outside, no light seemed to penetrate the thick, walls which from what anyone's best guess were made of layers of rotting wood, stone and metal sheeting. There were never any windows that opened, or any breeze that blew in. Only a single sliver of light during the day that barely peered in through a joint it the top corner of their room. She had no sense of time, no real sense of day or night. Some days for reasons she did not understand there was little or no light at all. To her, the world outside didn't exist. It was just something that might as well have been a dream, a fantastic imagination.

And yet, somewhere deep inside her chest—though she could not name it—something stirred.

There were others. Three women. They shared her prison, although no words passed between them. Their eyes, hollow and ringed with purple, flickered now and then in her direction but never stayed. They sat mostly in silence, folded into themselves, like statues halfway buried in the dust. Sometimes one of them would rock, back and forth, rhythmically, and the sound of that slow movement—skin against stone, breath against quiet—would fill the room in a strange lullaby of despair.

She mimicked it, it gave her a sense of ease, reliable routine that moved her mind off other thoughts.

V.F. Gingerelli

The rocking seemed to ease the tension in her shoulders. The girl had long since stopped hoping for comfort, but instinct drew her toward mimicry, toward movement. She rocked herself gently and felt, perhaps for the first time, that her body was hers to command.

Sometimes, when she wasn't rocking, she would wander the perimeter of the room. Her steps were slow and tentative, her bare feet imprinting faint tracks into the dirt. She would gaze upward, toward that crack in the ceiling where daylight sometimes poured in, thin and golden like the smallest sliver of hope. She would lift her small, grubby hands toward it, her fingers trembling in the light.

She would pinch the skin on her arm. Hard.

Just to feel something. To know she was real.

Her skin bore bruises, though she didn't know why. She did not understand injury as a concept. She did not associate pain with punishment. Pain was simply there, like cold air or hunger. She had never known life without it, and so it didn't frighten her. It was only another thing that existed.

She had no name. He called her "Girl." That was all she had ever been.

Girl, at My Window

He called them "Woman." Three of them.

This place smelled—always smelled—of rot. A mix of dampness and dust, mingled with the faint scent of something sour that hung in the air, heavy, like it had been there for years.

In the corner of the room a rusted green pipe slowly dripped water into a bucket. The pipe dripped all day and all night, and the best part of the day was the morning when the bucket had filled and four of them had a drink from what they had saved by not drinking the night before. They had to make sure to share or else run out of water, a problem especially when the summer air cooked their room and the dirt beneath their feet until the sun finally set in the evening.

On rare occasion one of the women would use their wet rough hand to wipe the dirt from her face. Other than this, there was no interaction, she might as well have been alone.

The corners of the room were filled with cobwebs, each strand glistening faintly, like a thousand forgotten threads that no one had cared enough about. She sometimes felt like those webs hanging, useless, not even enough food for the spiders to make a home. The floor not much of a floor at all but the stamped dirt and footprints of those pacing for years within. The walls were cracked, stained, peeling away in places, as if they, too, were withering under the weight of years of neglect. There was no color, no vibrancy, no life here. Just shadows and silence.

She didn't know what this place was or why she was here. The concept of "wrong" was as foreign as "freedom." Her entire sense of reality had been stolen from her before it could ever form.

And yet, like the spider that spun its web in the corner of the ceiling, she had survived.

Occasionally, there was a noise from the other side of the door. A shuffle, a distant murmur, footsteps that would stop and then fade away. For her, those were the most exciting times, if exciting was even the right feeling, she wouldn't know. Usually, the noise behind the door meant the good thing had arrived.

On the good days, there was food. Even though she didn't know what to call it, when the light stopped coming though the small crack in the roof, a small door would slide open and slide shut. A dirty metal tray would arrive and on it, a gift. She didn't know that it was food, or how it was needed for her body to survive, but she knew it was the best part of her day.

Girl, at My Window

The food was always strange. Scraps. Clumps of rice fused together into chalky lumps. Vegetables that no longer had color. Pieces of stale bread that flaked when touched, each bite gritty and hard. Sometimes, there was a sliver of cold, tough, and stringy meat, as if it had been forgotten for days.

It smelled wrong. But it filled her stomach. So, she ate.

That moment was always the same. A pause in the silence, a shift of weight as each woman in the room stirred slightly—like animals scenting water in the distance. No words were spoken, but each understood this was a good moment, the best they would have that day. The only one.

When the women were done, she would crawl to the tray and pick off whatever she could. They never fought her. They never acknowledged her. She was no threat. Just a shadow in the corner. A ghost.

She was small, too small even for the world that she had been forgotten by. A five-year-old girl, unkempt and thin, with tangled hair that hung in knots around her face, her clothes so dirty and worn they seemed to meld into the grime that covered the floor, camouflaging her, as if she wasn't invisible enough already. Day in and day out, she sat, her knees were pulled up to her chest, her arms wrapped around them, as she rocked back and forth in silence, surrounded by the others that occupied the space.

And yet… she was alive.

Every few days—though she had no measure for how often—another kind of sound would come. A heavier one. Boots. A thudding presence behind the door. This was not the good sound. This was the sound that made the air in the room colder, the shadows deeper.

The women would lower their heads.

She didn't know why. She only felt the shift in the room, the way everything seemed to freeze around her. That was when he would come.

He didn't say much. Just one word.

"Woman."

He would choose. One of them. Without ceremony. Without delay.

She didn't know what happened after that. Only that the chosen woman would return with a different weight in her eyes. Sometimes she would tremble. Sometimes she would weep without tears. But always, she was changed.

Girl, at My Window

The girl watched everything. Observed. Recorded, in a way that wasn't conscious but was complete.

There were no memories from before. Her life began here. With the pipe, the door, the three women, and Him.

Her mind was sharp, but unformed. Like a mirror without reflection.

Escape was not a possibility. There was nowhere else to be. The door had never opened for her, not once. He never said her name—only "Girl," with the edge of warning when she wandered too close to the door.

This was all the girl knew. She didn't know what it felt like to laugh with other children or to run through grass under the warmth of the sun. She didn't know the taste of fresh fruit, the smell of rain, or the sound of birds singing in the morning. She didn't know what a mother or a father were, didn't know the safety of being held, or the comfort of a voice saying her name with love. She only knew silence. Her world, every inch of it, was silence, and her only company was the faint hum of her own breath in the empty room. She knew nothing, but it was nothing that she knew and for now that would do.

Still, she wondered.

V.F. Gingerelli

Was there something beyond the crack in the roof? Where did the light go when it left the room?

Once, she saw something move there. A flicker of color—a bird, maybe. She didn't know the word for it, but it filled her with something close to wonder. The shape was unlike anything in the room. It flitted and was gone. But it stayed with her, nestled somewhere in her chest, like an ember she didn't know how to feed.

Her fingers would drift to the wall, tracing the cracks in the concrete, wondering if maybe—just maybe—there was something behind it. Something more.

But no one told her stories. No one told her anything.

When she pressed her ear to the ground, she could sometimes feel a vibration. Like the heartbeat of something large and distant. A world she could not see but knew existed.

Her ears were sharp. She could hear the smallest creak, the quietest sigh. Once, she thought she heard crying through the wall. She wasn't sure. It could have been a rat. Or the wind. She listened for hours afterward, trying to hear it again. But the room gave her nothing.

Sometimes, when she wasn't rocking, She would stand up and wander aimlessly around the room. Her feet left

Girl, at My Window

small prints on the floor as she moved through the stagnant air. She would walk in circles, tracing the same paths repeatedly. She would stop at to gaze at the spiders' webs or small speck of light glistening in and, lift her small trying to capture the light just to see what it would feel like.

There were nights—if you could call them that—when she would lie awake, staring at the ceiling, her arms wrapped around her thin legs. She didn't sleep often. The dreams, when they came, were strange and loud. Not frightening, just confusing. Shapes and colors she didn't understand.

The women didn't sleep either. Not really. They dozed. Rested. But never deeply. Their eyes always seemed to flicker open at the smallest sound. They lived in a permanent state of waiting.

And so, in the middle of this forgotten place, she sat.

Until one day, a mouse crept into the room and scampered across the floor in the darkness.

Almost too dark to even recognize its features.

It was the first living thing she'd ever seen that wasn't human.

V.F. Gingerelli

It darted across the floor, nose twitching, eyes bright. She watched it with rapt attention. The way it moved—quick and sure, as though it knew something she didn't. As if it had seen the world and had chosen, briefly, to visit her.

She didn't try to catch it. She simply followed it with her eyes.

Without a trace it disappeared.

And then, for the first time in her life, she had a thought that was entirely her own.

There is more than this place. The thought frightened her. But also—it lit something in her.

And suddenly, she looked at the cracks in the wall differently. She looked at the light through the ceiling as more than just light. She began to notice the small things. The rust patterns on the pipe. The way the dirt near the wall felt different than the center of the room. Softer. Less compacted.

That night, as the others sat unmoving, she moved her small fingers into the dirt near the wall.

Not with any real purpose. Just… to see.

Girl, at My Window

She didn't know what this was, who they all were or, what this place meant. She had been robbed in the most disgusting possible way. Nothing to long for, nothing to miss, no chance to explore the wonder of the world. Girl, woman, him was what her life encompassed. She didn't understand how long she had been in this room.

How many days had passed, how many nights had come and gone. There was no clock. There was no sound from the outside world, nothing to measure time by. Her only sense of time came from the hollow emptiness in her stomach when she was hungry or the weariness in her legs when she had sat too long. But hunger was just something that existed, like the dirt on the floor. It didn't mean anything. It was just there, a part of her existence that had always been there, just like the walls besides her and the floor beneath her.

When her fingers touched the dirt, her mind moved back and forth between hope and despair, sitting, waiting for something, anything.

V.F. Gingerelli

Him

"Woman," he said, his voice flat and commanding, echoing in the silence. The door creaked open on its warped metal hinges with a long, agonizing groan. It wasn't a loud noise, but in that sealed, tomb-like place, every sound reverberated like thunder. The flickering, stale light from the corridor behind him poured across the threshold and clung to the outlines of the women hunched in the shadows like frightened animals.

He didn't look at her—he never did. His eyes scanned the room quickly, calculated, indifferent. He pointed. One finger. No words of comfort, no invitation, just a single gesture toward one of the women slumped against the peeling, damp wall. His boots thudded against the packed dirt floor, each step a warning, a promise of inevitability.

Girl, at My Window

The chosen woman trembled. Not visibly—she had learned to hide that—but internally, her bones screamed. She rose on shaking legs, eyes cast down, never meeting his. She moved like a puppet pulled by strings, her soul buried somewhere too deep to retrieve. He gripped her arm roughly, not violently but firmly, as one might grip a sack of grain or an old broom—useful for now, easily discarded later.

The other women didn't flinch. They didn't speak. Silence was survival here.

She watched it all—every flick of his wrist, every breath, every blink—without moving a muscle. From her corner, knees drawn to her chest, she watched with the detached fascination of someone who didn't yet understand fear the way adults do. Not because she lacked emotion, but because her existence had never allowed her to learn the nuance of hope or the luxury of dreading its loss.

The woman was led away like so many times before. The heavy door shut behind them with a finality that made the air still again. The light was gone. He was gone. But something in the room shifted. The silence wasn't as complete as it had been.

She wasn't sure where the women went, it wasn't important to her. It didn't matter . She had long since stopped wondering about the world beyond the door. She had long since given up hope that anything outside of this place would ever make any sense to her. They would leave and then stumble in and return as he pushed them through the door and slammed it shut just as quick. It was always in silence, always acting as if nothing had changed. No words were exchanged between them, and the stillness would return to its quiet, heavy oppression. The door remained shut and they remained the same.

They disappeared, swallowed by whatever lay beyond the door. Some minutes passed, time twisted strangely in the stillness of that place but, the time they were gone never seemed that long. The woman returned, alone and sank back into her place among them, eyes vacant, lips pressed in a line that trembled ever so slightly. No words passed between them. They never did. It was as if nothing had happened. And yet, they all knew something unspeakable had happened. Something had been taken, or maybe something more had been lost each time they left the room.

The women came and went, the light came and went, and it seemed everyone, everything, seemed to being part of something.

Except for her.

Girl, at My Window

They had a role, something to do, something that placed them outside of the room. They had a purpose, even if it was a cold one.

But her? She was nothing.

No one spoke to her, no one acknowledged her. She was there, but she wasn't part of anything. She was just a fixture in the corner, sitting silently, watching as the world around her continued to move, even if that movement was just the silent opening and closing of the door.

The girl didn't fully understand what had occurred, only that this happened often, and that whatever it was, it always left the women quieter, paler, smaller. Something about them seemed to fade a little more each time they left and returned.

He was different. She wasn't afraid of him in the way the others were—not exactly. He brought food. He opened the door. He was the only connection to the world beyond the gray. In her mind, distorted by years of solitude and deprivation, he was… not kind, but not cruel either. Simply necessary. He was the only figure who ever acknowledged her presence at all, and even then, only to say one word.

"Girl," he would bark, not with malice, but with irritation, pointing sharply toward the corner if she wandered too close to the door or to one of the women. Like training a dog to heel. His voice didn't carry warmth or venom—only control, absolute and unfeeling.

She had learned quickly. Back to the corner. Head down. Stillness was safety.

In those moments, her breath would catch in her throat—not out of panic, but out of uncertainty. Would he take her, too? Would she be chosen like the women? Would he ever say "Girl" and beckon her toward the door rather than away from it?

He never did.

And so, she remained a non-existent fixture in the room. Present, yet untouched. Watching, always watching. The women didn't acknowledge her. Not out of cruelty, but out of a kind of shared numbness. Their spirits had been fractured so many times, stitched together with silence and fear. There was no room left in their minds to make space for her.

She had no name—only "Girl." No identity. Just a shape in the corner. But she was learning, piecing together her world through sounds and gestures, light and shadow.

Girl, at My Window

He never stayed long. His body moved like it hurt to be inside it—every step slow and strained. He limped slightly, favoring his left leg, though he never made a sound to suggest pain. His clothes hung loose from his frame. His hair, was cropped close to his head, revealing the pinkish scar that stretched from his brow to the corner of his hairline. It looked like a tear in the skin that had never healed properly.

The scar fascinated her. In the half-light, it shimmered like a river of dull red. She had no word for pain beyond hunger and cold, but she wondered sometimes if it hurt him. If maybe that was why he never smiled, why his face always looked so heavy and closed.

But his eyes were what haunted her most. Not because they were cruel or kind, but because they seemed… empty. Although the color of them was nice, it was behind them, the story they told that is what gave her unease. His eyes didn't see people, only things to be used.

When he left, the silence would return like a fog settling thick over the room. The women would resume their stillness, sinking back into themselves like crumbling statues. She would curl up again in her corner, tracing the familiar cracks in the wall with her fingers, trying to make shapes out of the peeling paint.

V.F. Gingerelli

Sometimes, the silence felt heavier than his presence. At least when he came, there was movement. Sound. Something different, even if it brought fear. The silence was worse. It crept into her bones, into her thoughts, until even the idea of escape faded into static.

She had no memories of before this place. This room was her entire existence. Its smells—damp earth, rust, and mildew—were her air. Its texture—grit and rot and cold—was her touch. She had never known sunlight, not really. The sliver of it that came through the crack in the roof was like a dream she could barely reach. She would crawl toward it sometimes, stretching her fingers into its warmth. That light was the only thing that felt real, like a voice that hummed to her in a language she didn't know but instinctively trusted.

Once, she'd tried to hum back, and the sound had startled her so much she had clamped her mouth shut and hadn't tried again for days.

The others didn't hum. They didn't speak. They didn't cry. Whatever had been inside them had long since dried up, soaked into the walls.

But she was still young. She still had questions, even if she didn't know how to form them. And the biggest question she carried was this: *Why am I here?*

Girl, at My Window

Not in a philosophical sense. Not "Why me?" but literally, *what is this place?* Why were the walls so high and so dark? Why did the door only open for him? Why did the women go out and come back changed? Why did no one ever smile?

The room itself had a kind of quiet power over her. It was the world she knew, the only world she had ever known. The door never stayed open long enough for her to peer outside and glimpse what lay beyond. It was always closed, always a barrier between her and the unknown. The silence and stillness of the room had settled into her bones, and she no longer tried to imagine what lay outside. She was resigned to the fact that her life was here, within these four walls. She had no reason to believe anything would ever change. The room was her prison, but she had long since stopped hoping for escape. She had stopped hoping for anything at all.

She didn't have the words to ask. But the questions lived in her, thrumming beneath her ribs like the tiny heartbeat of a trapped bird.

She watched him differently than the women did. They flinched when he entered. She stared. When he dragged the women out, she sometimes took a few quiet steps forward, curious. That's when he would notice her and say it again: "Girl." The word always landed like a cold drop of water down her spine. She would retreat immediately, chastised.

But there was something in that moment—some flicker of attention—that felt oddly precious. He saw her. Not kindly, not warmly, but he saw her. And when you are invisible most of your life, even acknowledgment from a shadow can feel like sunlight.

Still, there was a line. She had learned not to cross it.

Each time he returned, she studied his face. Not just the scar or his eyes, but the way his jaw clenched when he spoke, the way his shoulders hunched when he walked. He was always alert, always looking. She wondered if he feared something—or someone—beyond the room. Maybe that's why he came and left so quickly. Maybe he, too, was hiding from something.

Sometimes, she imagined that he had a room like this one, somewhere else. A room where he sat on the floor and stared at the walls. A room where someone else told *him* where to sit, where to go. Could he be as lonely as they were? It made her feel strange—like pity, but she didn't know that word.

The other women, they more than this once, long ago. She was sure of it. Lives that had been lived through,

Girl, at My Window

sights and sounds they felt. They were different, they acted different than her, colder as if they longed for some missing piece they may never have again. But now, like her, they were nameless and without life. Voiceless and without choice.

Except for Him. He had a voice. And he used it like a whip.

"Woman."

"Girl."

He never said anything more.

And yet, in those two words, he shaped the tone of their lives in that place.

He was the gatekeeper of time, the harbinger of change, the master of their tiny world. They didn't know anything of his world either. They never asked. Some wounds don't bleed until you named them, called them out for everyone to see.

But still, she wondered. What was his story? Did he have one? Did anyone care enough to ask?

V.F. Gingerelli

He existed as both captor and constant. The force of change and the unchanging. He was always the same. Always in control.

But one day—perhaps not far from now—that might change.

It was as though she didn't belong anywhere else but there, in that corner. Her body, small and fragile, seemed to be too much for the rest of the room. It was as though the space didn't know what to do with her, and she didn't know what to do with it. The room felt like it was closing in on her, swallowing her slowly, with each passing minute. There was no room for hope here. No room for movement. No room for anything other than the corner where she sat and waited.

And so, the days melted together, indistinguishable and slow. Time had no meaning for her, just as the world beyond the door had no meaning. She didn't need to know anything else. It was cold. It was dark. It was empty. But it was all she had. She was lost, but she didn't know how to find herself. They had fallen so deep, and into a place, so dark, that they could find even the dullest light to guide out of the shadows.

Over and over again, the routine continued.

Girl, at My Window

And in the corner of the room, where light touched the floor and one small girl sat, a question bloomed.

What if this wasn't all there was?

V.F. Gingerelli

A New Friend

Door creaks.
Footsteps.
A tray shoved through the bottom slot.
A body taken.
A breath held.
A breath released.

>She lived by that rhythm.

>And then it would begin again.

Door creaks.
Footsteps.
A tray shoved through the bottom slot.
A body taken.

Girl, at My Window

A breath held.
A breath released.

     She didn't know who he was, not really was except a constant existence in their lives. He didn't smile. He didn't hurt her—not in ways she could explain. But every time his boots thudded across the floor, she stopped breathing. Her body froze. Her spirit shrank. And when the door closed behind him, the silence returned, heavier than before.

     He came like a shadow with a voice shaped like a blade.

"Woman."
"Girl."

     That was all he said. That was all he ever needed to say. His words didn't carry emotion. They carried *power.* And everyone obeyed.

     The room was always the same. Stale. Cold. Silent. But to the little girl, the silence had started to whisper. Her hands, small and pale, reached toward the walls as though they could somehow speak back. With each fingertip she traced the faded paint and crumbling edges, fascinated by the uneven texture beneath her touch. There was a quiet intimacy in the way she connected with the room, as if even its decaying walls might one day answer the questions she didn't know how to ask.

She didn't know what questions meant. Or dreams. Or time. But lately, something stirred in her. A presence. A flicker. A hint of something not quite belonging to the darkness.

The cracks along the wall were her stories. She'd trace them again and again, lips moving silently as though reciting forgotten names, forgotten paths, imagined escapes. Behind every fracture, every jagged line, she imagined there was something—anything—more than what this place offered. But those imaginings were secret. Fragile. Private. Because no one had ever told her that "outside" was real.

Her only companion was the raggedy doll, its fabric worn thin from endless handling, its seams fraying like old memories. Yet in that doll's sightless eyes, the girl found solace. It wasn't just a toy—it was her heart outside of her body. When she held it, she felt less alone. Less like a shadow and more like a person. It wasn't real in the way most people think of "real," but to her, the doll breathed. It *listened*.

The girl didn't know what it meant to be lonely. Loneliness was the air she breathed. But slowly, imperceptibly, a change was coming. A feeling foreign to her

Girl, at My Window

heart began to stir. Not joy, not hope exactly—something quieter, something older. An ache to be *seen*.

But one day, the rhythm faltered. A ripple in the silence.

The girl was tracing her usual path across the room, fingertips grazing the walls like always, when she stopped. Something... was different. Not in the room. Not in the walls. *In her.*

It started with a sound.

A tiny shuffle in the dirt.

She noticed the slight rustling sound in the corner of the room that didn't belong. It was barely perceptible, but to her, the absence of noise had made her attuned to even the faintest disturbance. Her small hands stilled their habitual motion of tracing the cracks in the wall, and she listened more intently. The sound wasn't the usual creaking of the building, nor the elements outside pressing against the roof. No, this was something alive, something moving with purpose. It was a subtle sound, that she could not quite put her finger on.

Curiosity, the one thing she still possessed, drew her toward the noise. She shuffled carefully across the floor, her

V.F. Gingerelli

feet brushing against the cold, gritty surface, the chill of the room still biting into her skin. As she reached the corner of the room, she paused, holding her breath, afraid the noise would stop if she moved too suddenly. She waited.

She had long since lost the ability to dream and had no understanding of what life could be like outside. The notion of a world full of people, of trees that had meaning, of laughter and warmth—it was alien to her. She could not fathom it. She couldn't even imagine it. All she knew was the silence, the cold, the dirt, and the darkness that had been with her as long as she could remember.

The rustling continued—soft, almost rhythmic, like a whisper too quiet to understand but too insistent to ignore. She crept forward, each step careful, each breath measured, her eyes straining in the dim light that spilled through the narrow crack in the ceiling like the ghost of daylight long forgotten. Dust shimmered faintly in that light, suspended in the air like particles of time itself.

She turned slowly. Her eyes caught movement—the mouse had returned!

It was a small, brown, fragile and deliberate creature that emerged from a jagged hole near the base of the wall. She stilled, every muscle frozen in reverence, as if the mouse's presence had suddenly rendered the room sacred. It

Girl, at My Window

was such a small creature, and yet it moved with purpose—as if unaware of the silence, the weight, the grief that hung in the air around them both. It moved without fear, its twitching nose exploring the ground, paws clutching a crumb so minuscule she hadn't even noticed it before. For the small mouse this must have been a feast.

Food well…hunger was a dull ache in her belly. A constant. She had never known fullness or warmth or meals. Hunger was simply part of her. Something to live beside. When it grew too sharp, she curled herself into a ball, pressing hands to her stomach until the ache faded into numbness. That was easier. Numbness was easier than feeling.

When it gnawed at her, she would sit down on the floor, curling into herself, her hands clutching her stomach. There were no meals, no warm food to fill her. There were no voices to comfort her, no parents to tell her that things would be okay. There was only the gnawing emptiness, the hollow feeling inside her, the quietness that filled the room as she waited for something that never came.

She didn't feel that now, she couldn't think of anything else. How could she when by chance this little creature wandered back into her life. This time she knew its presence wasn't a dream, it wasn't imagined.

V.F. Gingerelli

It was strange—no, it was *miraculous*.

She didn't scream. She didn't chase. She simply watched. Spellbound.

Its eyes were bright. Its body moved with purpose, slipping through the cracks in the room like it had always known the way out. It vanished in seconds. Gone. But it left behind something powerful.

A question.

The mouse didn't belong here in this hollow, forgotten place, just as she didn't. Its presence was an intrusion against despair, a reminder that the world still turned, even in hidden corners. Something stirred in her chest, uncoiling like a long-forgotten memory: a sense of outside. Of grass. Of wind that moved without walls to stop it. Of something green, or golden, or soft.

The mouse was real. Unmistakably alive. She could almost hear its heartbeat as it thudded like a secret song beneath its fur. And that aliveness, so fragile and yet so complete, pressed against the silence like a question—an invitation. It was proof, quietly and stubbornly enduring, that something waited beyond this place. That there were more than the cold walls, the heavy air, the endless gray.

Girl, at My Window

How did it get in? Where did it come from? Could I go too?

In that moment, she didn't just see a mouse. What many may have glanced past without a thought She saw hope—small, trembling, and unstoppable.

For the first time in her life, she had a thought that was truly hers. Not just reaction. Not just habit. *Wonder.*

There is more than this.

It was a dangerous idea. A dangerous feeling. She didn't know the word for "freedom," but something inside her had been lit. The mouse had *been* somewhere. It had *seen* something. She wanted that.

Later that day, the girl returned to the spot where the mouse had vanished. She got down on her knees and began to press her fingers into the dirt. It was softer here. Looser. The smell was different, too—damp, like the air had moved through here once.

And so she dug. Slowly. Cautiously. Not with a goal. Not yet. Just to *know.* The dirt gave way beneath her fingernails, tiny clumps falling aside, and her hands began to tremble—not from fear, but anticipation. She had no words for escape. No concept of freedom. But she *felt* something shift. Something small but seismic.

V.F. Gingerelli

That night, as the other women lay quiet, unmoving, the girl could not sleep. Her hands tingled. Her thoughts swirled. The mouse had shown her something. And she could not unsee it. The hole seemed impossibly new, and as if it had always been there, patiently waiting for her to finally see it.

It must have come from the outside, from somewhere beyond the room. She could feel that instinctively, as though the very presence of it carried the faint scent of something she had long forgotten—fresh air, perhaps, or the promise of something untouchable. For a long moment, she simply stared at the hole, her heart racing in her chest, her mind struggling to comprehend what this meant. Where did it go, where possibly could it go?

Could it be that there was more beyond the walls? Could it be the things she imagined, those things that would seem may never be, could be closer than she had ever realized?

Light shown in, just sliver of it, impossibly narrow, spilled into the room from high above where a crack in the ceiling refused to be covered. It came and went, gentle but faithful. On good days, it stretched across the dirt floor and kissed the girl's bare toes. Even when it was dim and dull it eventually came back in all its brilliance peering into the small crack in the roof, almost smiling on her. Sometimes, She

Girl, at My Window

would talk to the light, her voice barely a whisper, as if she was hoping that someone, something, would listen.

She had grown to love that light. Sometimes she would sit and talk to it, whispering fragments of thought like confessions—half-hopes and almost-words. Could this be the place the mouse came from, could they be connected?

Her new friend's intrusion had cracked the silence in a way she hadn't thought possible. It had made her existence feel larger, the walls a little less imposing. For the first time in as long as she could remember, she didn't feel so entirely alone.

She bent down slowly, examining the hole more closely. It was small, barely large enough for the mouse to slip through, but it was there, a gap in the structure of the room. Her fingers grazed the edges of the hole, feeling the roughness of the jagged plaster and the thinness of the space beyond. She pressed harder, wishing she could break through, to see what lay behind the wall. There was no way of knowing, but the thought of the world on the other side stirred something deep inside her—a longing, a pull toward something she couldn't name.

Days passed—or maybe weeks. Time had no face here. Only rhythm. Silence. The occasional mutter of pain

V.F. Gingerelli

from one of the women in the dark. But then, something else changed.

The girls comforting meeting with this new stranger was an epiphany—there was something more, something beyond the room. There was something out there. She had never imagined such a possibility. She had always accepted the silence, the stillness, as the only truth. The door had always been closed, a permanent boundary between her and the unknown. But now, with the mouse, she realized that the barrier wasn't as impenetrable as she had thought. There was a way out—if not for her, then at least for the mouse. The hole was small, but it was a way forward, a way beyond.

She sank back into the corner, her knees drawn to her chest, the cold pressing in around her like a second skin. But her mind would not rest. It spun with images of the mouse—its quick, precise movements, the flick of its tail, and most of all, that hole. That impossibly small opening in the wall, so ordinary and yet humming with possibility. She couldn't stop thinking about it. What lay beyond? Was it just another space like the one they were now, or something more—something free, something untouched by this place?

The thought dug into her like a splinter. That tiny creature, weightless and unnoticed, had shown her something she'd long buried: the chance of escape. Of change. Of *outside*. The mouse hadn't hesitated. It had moved with certainty,

Girl, at My Window

with purpose. And that hole—it hadn't just been a passage for the mouse. It had become a symbol, a map carved in silence, pointing toward something she had barely allowed herself to believe in anymore.

Her chest tightened. She didn't know what she would find if she followed. Maybe it was nothing. But even nothing new, just something different, felt less suffocating than the endless gray stillness she'd been breathing for so long. For the first time in what felt like a lifetime, she let the thought take root, wild and dangerous: *what if there was more?*

A tremor passed through her. She couldn't wait. Not now. Not after seeing it.

In the thick silence, with no voices, no eyes watching—just her and the pulse of hope beating louder than her fear—she reached forward. Slowly, deliberately, she began to claw at the packed dirt, fingers scraping against the ground, every movement quiet but determined. Her nails cracked, the soil cool and stubborn, but beneath it—she could smell it. Something nearly unfamiliar, sweet, faintly damp, and alive. A scent she had no memory for, only instinct. It called to something inside her.

She didn't look back. The mouse would not return. It had already given her what she needed.

V.F. Gingerelli

And now—now it was her turn to follow.

Girl, at My Window

The Only Child

After packing a small picnic basket, the Bryan, Lynn and Emma headed out to the park. Emma held her mother's hand, her fingers wrapped around Lynn's warm, reassuring grip. As they walked, Emma noticed the way the leaves shimmered in the wind and how the air smelled of fresh grass and earth. It was a good day, a peaceful day, the kind that felt like it was made just for her.

At the park, Bryan found a quiet spot near the pond, where the trees created a natural canopy of shade. Emma settled down on the soft blanket that her mother had spread out, and for a few moments, she simply sat there, letting her mind wander. She watched the ripples on the water, the ducks paddling in the pond, and the occasional squirrel darting up a tree. The world around her was alive, yet there was a stillness to it, a calmness that Emma found comforting.

As Bryand and Lynn unpacked the picnic basket, Emma noticed a group of children playing near the swings. Her emotions stirred.

"Mommy" Emma said with hesitation, "Do you think my sister will be here soon?"

Lynn looked at Bryan and with hesitation and sadness replied, "Were doing our best, we hope so!" Trying to put this innocent line of questioning out of their mind Lynn and Bryan focused their energies on the beautiful day ahead of them.

They were laughing and running, playing near the animals and imagining the most wonderful stories to tell each other. Emma glanced at her parents, who were busy setting out the sandwiches and fruit, talking quietly amongst themselves when just then a mouse ran by her feet. Emma's attention immediately shifted as she watched it scurry away.

The day at the park was supposed to be a respite from the heaviness of everything. Emma's laughter echoed in the air as she ran between the trees, chasing after squirrels or pretending to be a bird soaring through the sky. For a moment, all the frustration and heartache that had been

Girl, at My Window

quietly building behind closed doors seemed miles away. But as the sun warmed her back and the rustling leaves created a gentle melody, a subtle tension began to rise, lingering in the air between Emma's parents. It was the kind of tension they couldn't shake, even on days that seemed so perfect.

For the past two years, Lynn and Bryan had been doing every to give Emma a sibling. Having and raising the baby was supposed to be hard, making the baby, at least the first part was not, or at least that is the way it seemed. Everyone around her was having children of their own, making families, fulfilling lifelong dreams. These dreams had once seemed so simple, so attainable, but now had turned into a long, drawn-out ordeal. Three rounds of IVF, and three rounds of hope and failure. And now, with each failed attempt, the air in their home grew a little colder, the spaces between them a little wider.

Lynn's frustration was palpable. She couldn't understand why this was happening to her, why, after everything she had been through, she couldn't conceive. She had always imagined that this part of life would be easy—that becoming a mother again would be a natural progression. But each failed cycle of IVF left her feeling more confused, more disappointed, and increasingly disconnected from her identity. What was wrong with her? What had she done to deserve this endless spiraling cycle of disappointment?

V.F. Gingerelli

Bryan was her rock, the steady presence that was always there, always loving. He didn't know what to say to ease her pain—nothing seemed to work, he could not fix this broken dream, no matter what they did, what new step they tried. But he tried and would keep trying. He held her when the tears came, he reassured her when she sank into doubt. He would tell her, time and again, that they were in this together. That no matter what happened, they would still have each other and Emma. But the words never felt like enough.

Lynn's mind was a whirlwind of conflicting emotions—guilt, shame, anger, and a deep, aching sense of helplessness. She had always been the strong one, the person who could handle everything life threw at her, but this—this was different. She couldn't control it, and it was eating her up from the inside.

Bryan understood, or at least, he tried to. His love for Lynn was unconditional, but even he was struggling. They had spent so much money on the treatments. It had drained their savings, leaving them with little more than the hope that the next round would finally work. And each time, when it didn't, the disappointment was almost too much to bear. They had hoped for so long, but now it felt as though they had nothing left to give.

Girl, at My Window

The tension between them was subtle, but it was always there, consistent.

Lynn would withdraw into herself, retreating to a quiet corner of their home, her eyes distant and full of sadness. Bryan would try to reach out, offering support, but it often felt like he was walking on eggshells, afraid to say the wrong thing or make her feel worse.

At night, as they lay in bed together, the silence between them was thick with unspoken words. There was no more talk of plans, of trying again. The dream of expanding their family felt like a distant memory, a dream that no longer felt attainable. They were both exhausted, emotionally and physically drained from the cycle of hope and loss. Sleep was less and less satisfying, dates and outings less and less enjoyable.

Intimate times felt like a chore, growingly more useless and devoid of passion. The love between them was still there, but it was clouded by the overwhelming weight of disappointment and the uncertainty of what their future held.

Bryan and Lynn did everything they could, tried all possible routes, gave all they had and they still were not enough.

V.F. Gingerelli

Amid it all, Emma was oblivious to the strain her parents were under. She continued to laugh and play, her world still bright and full of wonder. But Lynn couldn't help but feel a pang of guilt when she saw the way Emma eagerly asked if her sister would be arriving soon. How could she explain to her little girl that the hope they had held onto for so long had slowly begun to slip away? How could she tell Emma that they had tried everything, but it seemed as though the universe had other plans for them?

"Mommy, do you think my sister will be here soon?" Emma had asked that next morning, her voice filled with innocent hope.

Lynn's heart clenched. She glanced at Bryan, searching for some kind of reassurance, but all she found in his eyes was the same sadness she felt. He squeezed her hand gently, trying to offer some comfort, but Lynn knew the truth. They were running out of time, running out of money, running out of hope.

"We're doing our best, we hope so," Lynn replied, as she had so many times in the past few years. She forced a smile, but the words felt hollow.

Emma didn't seem to notice the tension. She was busy running through the grass, or playing in her room, chasing after her imagination. But Lynn couldn't shake the

Girl, at My Window

feeling that these carefree days weren't enough to mask the growing divide between her and Bryan, the growing divide between the life they had once dreamed of and the life they were now living.

"We will figure this out," Bryan reassured her.

Lynn almost shrugged off his comment, she had heard it many times before, it carried almost no weight. "We have tried everything, we have always wanted another child, Emma has always wanted a brother or sister."

Lynn continued, "I just feel so desperate."

Bryan, ever the optimist, never seemed to waver. He held onto the belief that things would work out—that they would find a way to make it happen. Lynn understood his optimistic approach, but it remained an annoyance. She sometimes even yearned for him to break down, to scream, so that she knew the pain she felt was understood and shared by him.

Even he had his moments of doubt. He could see how worn-out Lynn was, how drained she had become. He could see the way her eyes had lost some of their spark, the way the frustration bubbled just beneath the surface. He wanted to fix it, wanted to take away her pain, but he didn't know how.

V.F. Gingerelli

Lynn couldn't shake the feeling that things were changing in ways she couldn't control. She had hoped that this day would provide the clarity she needed, the space to heal, but it only seemed to magnify the cracks in their relationship.

Every failed attempt felt like another blow; another dream shattered. She had poured so much of herself into this process, and now, the cost of it all seemed too high. Lynn had tried to be patient. She had told herself that it would happen when the time was right, that maybe there was a reason for everything. But as the months passed and each attempt ended in disappointment, the doubt crept in. Maybe they weren't meant to have another child. Maybe Emma was the only child they were ever going to have. And if that was the case, then what did that mean for them as a family? What did that mean for her and Bryan?

Bryan frequently noticed Lynn's silence and, as he wrapped his arm around her shoulders, pulling her close to offer comfort he said, "Someday, sometime we will understand why this is happening, we WILL be whole as a family, I believe it."

The weight of those words between them pressed heavier on her chest. What would tomorrow bring? Would they continue to try, or would they finally have to accept that their family was already complete? For now, there was no answer. Only the uncertainty of what lay ahead, and the hope that, somehow, they would find a way to move forward together.

V.F. Gingerelli

A Fixture

The morning light was dim, as usual, creeping in through the crack in the ceiling, casting its pale glow onto the floor of the room. The girl sat, motionless, in the corner, her fingers grazing the jagged hole beneath the wall. The tiny opening, now no larger than a fist, where fresh air breathed the smallest bit of life into the room, still seemed an impossibility to her—like a crack in the very fabric of reality, a glimpse into something beyond the walls that had been her prison for so long.

    She had spent the night contemplating it, feeling the roughness of the plaster with her fingertips, tracing its edges over and over, as if hoping it would reveal more, as if hoping she could find a way to break free to whatever adventure there was on the outside.

Girl, at My Window

In the silence, her breath became shallow with anticipation.

"What is it," she said, "was there more than this dark, and dusty space?"

The mouse had shown her there was a way out. If it could slip through, why couldn't she?

But as the sun began its slow climb, casting long shadows across the barren room, the girl's attention was drawn away from hope and inspiration of something else beyond their room. A soft groan echoed from across the room. She blinked, squinting into the half-darkness, her heart quickening. It was one of the women, something was happening that she would never forget. Something was happening, a catalyst that would ignite a series of events the girl could not imagine in her wildest dreams.

One of the three women was lying on the floor, her thin body curled into a shape that looked unnatural, as though she was trying to escape the weight of the air itself. She didn't have a name as far as anyone knew, the only one who spoke was him and when he did seldom speak "woman" or, "girl" was the only thing he ever said.

The girl didn't understand what was happening, but she knew the woman was sick. They all were. Every day, her coughs had grown worse, her skin paler, her movements more lethargic. Their bodies grew smaller and their bones more pronounced. Their room was cold, damp and dirty, their hair knotted. They did nothing, said nothing because if they did the energy from the little food they were given would be wasted on trivial things.

She did not know why or what they were doing in that dark place. There was nothing but what *this* was, whatever that meant. The girl had noticed the changes in the women, just as she had noticed the changes in herself. The silence had become heavier, more oppressive. It was as though their bodies were giving in to the stillness, each one of them slowly fading under the weight of the walls. They had been there for as long as she could remember, yet she didn't know their names—only their faces, their features, and the way they had come to resemble the room itself. They may have been merely fixtures, lifeless with no greater purpose than to be used at will and, just like those lifeless fixtures they had no say, no reason or understanding of their purpose or what else remained of life.

The women had all been there before her, trapped in the same hopeless cycle, each of them lost in the darkness, each of them suffering in ways the girl didn't fully understand. The girl only believed that they like her, only ever knew this room; knew that this was how we all lived, there was nothing more. The woman was writhing in discomfort,

Girl, at My Window

her breath shallow and rapid, the girl felt an unfamiliar sense of unease stir in her chest.

Just then the woman's body stilled. For a moment, the room felt quieter, colder as if an air of absence creeped in the cracks of the walls. Even the light through the ceiling seemed to dampen. The day drew long, longer than any day before and, although there was never a sound to be heard in that room it seemed so quiet that you may have even heard the dust as it floated across your face. After a time that stretched longer than it should have, the girl heard Him. Her heartbeat as fast as it could, it was as if she could see it forcing her chest up and down.

The door to the room creaked open, and she could hear him moving in. He always carried a strange presence that seemed to suck the air out of the room. His footsteps, heavy and methodical, approached the room. The girl didn't know what would happen next. She had learned early on that it was best not to make a sound when he came. She put her head in her lap and sat silently in the corner of the room where she would remain for most of the day. It was safer to stay invisible, to remain as still as the walls themselves.

When he entered, He pointed and said, "woman."

Just then in a flash the girl had seen something that she had never imagined. His eyes darted to the corner of the room where the woman's lifeless body lay. He looked upon her body and, with eyebrows furrowed and a crooked smirk in one corner of his mouth he blew a loud puff of air from his nose, shook his head and entered the room. He looked at nothing but was visibly annoyed…he stripped her shirt and pants, taking no care as he ripped them from her body. The clothes were thrown in the center of the room.

This lasted for merely a minute, but that minute drew on for what lasted like a day. He stood up, reached down and groaned as he grabbed her dark, knotted hair and dragged her bruised pale body from the room. The girl's eyes followed; her breath almost cutting her throat as it escaped her body. She wasn't sure what to feel—there was relief in her, a strange feeling that perhaps the woman's suffering had finally ended, but there was also fear, the unsettling certainty that the same fate awaited them all. Just then, the door slammed and without a word she was gone.

Once she had been taken, the silence settled back into the room like an oppressive weight. The girl could hear the faint rustling of the other women as they stirred. It was a silence filled with confusion, nerves, fear, and a strange, silent understanding.

The two remaining women did not speak, but their eyes met, full of unsaid questions, unsaid fears. The girl felt them watching her and just then something happened,

Girl, at My Window

something that left the girl with more questions than answers. Something that was even more confusing than what had happened minutes before.

V.F. Gingerelli

The *Other* Door

Emma was a bright girl, whose blonde hair was always brushed and floated in the breeze as she ran through their home, playing and imagining all of life's possibilities. Her eyes were as blue as the morning sky, she knew nothing about the darkness of the world and felt safe, cuddled, cozy in bed at night. They lived in a beautiful little home in a row of houses nestled at the edge of a small town, surrounded by the most beautiful fields and forests.

      Inside, everything was warm and full of love — the scent of chocolate chip cookies often drifted from the kitchen, her dog Gus was always at her heels, and laughter echoed through the rooms like music. Emma had everything a child could dream of, a cozy bed, complete with bedtime stories whispered by her mother, a fluffy dog full of more kisses than anyone needed and, a heart so full of joy it seemed nothing could ever dim its light.

Each morning, Emma would run barefoot through the dewy grass, chasing butterflies and pretending the world was her kingdom, without a care in the world. An activity taken for granted only by a child. Her days were spent with crayons, picture books, and little adventures in the backyard, where every flower and stone had a name and a story. She had her weekly drawing routine with her dad and played chase with her dog.

She had never known pain, nor fear, nor sorrow. Her life was a simple symphony of love and wonder, and even the rain felt like something magical. To everyone who saw her, Emma was the very picture of innocence, sheltered in a world built carefully by the love of her parents. And so should each child be, until, at a time, unfortunately, life's myths of perfection come crashing down upon us all.

Change, as it often does, came quietly and without warning. In the days to come, she would face something that was equally as confusing as it was fearful. And though she didn't know it yet, Emma's world was about to become something entirely different.

V.F. Gingerelli

They had always been there, just as she had always been there—yet they had never truly seen her. No words had passed between them, no comfort offered, only the quiet rhythm of their shared misery and the unspoken fear of Him. But now, something had shifted. Moments after the room fell silent, tears began to stream from the eyes of the woman in the corner. The girl didn't understand it, but the tears spoke of sorrow, frustration, and confusion. It was something she had never witnessed before—a feeling, an act, utterly foreign to her.

Without pause or concern, the girl rose slowly and began to move. Her bare feet brushed against the cold dirt floor.

As she moved toward the corner of the room, she took a hesitant step and suddenly locked eyes with the crying woman.

For a moment she was shaken, frozen by the interaction and then almost in the same breath immediately thrust forward by a rock that had lodged itself into the middle of her foot.

As she tripped as her head came crashing down against the wall.

Girl, at My Window

The women watched her their faces were gaunt and hollow, but in a split moment of indecision decided to rise, their movements were slow and deliberate, they were so weak from the brutish treatment of their captor they needed to be careful to conserve their energy. They both rose and helped the girl from the wall. As the girl got to her feet a small cut sent blood trickling down her forehead where she hit her head.

The woman grabbed the shirt in the middle of the room wiped the blood and said, "Now, now, everything will be okay, it's not that bad."

The woman tossed the blood-soaked shirt to the corner of the room.

She was a tall woman with dark-hair and sunken eyes. Her voice was cracked, weak, but there was a tremor in it that carried with it a strange air of concern and excitement.

"You found something, didn't you?" Her voice barely carried across the room, but the girl understood, and the other woman who had heard the conversation proceeded to crawl on hands and knees across the room.

The girl nodded, her heart racing. She didn't know why she was sharing this moment with them, why for the first time she had heard more words than any other time in her life. There was something in the woman's eyes—they were wide open and although the dirt wore thick on her skin and her cheekbones protruded all the same something was different almost as if the glimmer of light that shown through the crack in the ceiling had filled her face with warm and hope.

The woman knelt shakily; her hands pressed against her knees for support. She approached the wall of the room cautiously, as though afraid that the discovery of the hole was some kind of illusion.

"You—can you feel it?" the woman asked, her voice trembling. "Do you think... it's a way out?"

The girl didn't respond immediately. She didn't know what to say. Could it be? A way out? A way out where? The mouse had shown her the hole, but she had no way of knowing where it led. It was just a small opening in the wall. Yet, there was something in the air—a feeling of possibility that the girl hadn't felt before. It was like a spark, a faint warmth that somehow contrasted with the coldness of the room.

The dark-haired woman instantly lay as flat as possible, moving quicker than the girl had ever seen anyone move. She pressed her face against the whole and breathed in as much air from the space between the floor and the wall.

Girl, at My Window

With lungs full of crisp spring air, the woman exhaled and let out an albeit quiet but cheerful sigh.

Both women now crowded around the corner of the room, their intrigue filled the room making even the dust from the dirt floor rise from the floor and buzz with possibility.

In a quiet and serious tone, the woman told the girl, "It is time, we must get out, or we'll be just like her and never see the world again."

The girl knew this had to do with the whole in the wall. She was puzzled what possibility it held, what was the world, why now did the women decide to speak so many words. For the longest time the girl heard no words but only groans and quiet and still. She had many thoughts, she had ideas but no way to express them, she had never been exposed to the conversation, the delights and joys that most others take for granted.

V.F. Gingerelli

Risky Business

The woman moved closer, crawling slowly across the room. Her body was frail, every motion carved from exhaustion, but her voice was strong.

"My name is Isla," the dark hair woman said to the girl.

The girl tilted her head.

"What is Isla," the girl hesitantly asked.

"It's a name. My name. What people call me."

The girl blinked. Finally, she understood, and proclaimed with joy, "oh like I am girl!"

Girl, at My Window

Isla reached out, gently covering the girl's mouth with her palm. One could see the visible fear in her face. Isla knew that she was not to blame for this excitement. For so long they sat in that place, silent. Breathing the same air, eating the same food, drinking the same water but never interacting.

"Shhh... not too loud. He might come." Her voice was trembling now. But not with fear. With urgency.

"You're not 'girl.' That's not your name. You just don't know it yet."

The girl blinked again. Something in her chest squeezed tightly. She wasn't girl. She was *a* girl. But not "Girl." She had never felt more real.

Isla removed her hand from the girl's mouth, "you need to be very quiet," "always." She continued, "He may come back, we don't ever want him to come back."

The girl did not understand he brough food, he helped us and except for once he always brought the women back here. He was good and the girl felt safe.

Now the two women had gathered around the girl and the mouse sized whole in the wall, they stared at the packed dirt that had been under their feet for the years they had occupied the cell sized room. Darkness filled the room and though there was not much to see they could feel the warmth and presence surrounded by one another for the first time. They had felt, even breathed in the air that came through that opening. They had never imagined that they would be able to make their way through the base of the wall, like every other structure a foundation would have prevented it. That small creature showed them at least it was a possibility worth exploring if it meant their freedom.

    The third woman, Jane, joined them then. Jane was smaller, quieter, but with a fire in her eyes. She stared at the patch of disturbed earth beside the wall, her expression unreadable.

    "You found something," she said. "Didn't you?"

    The girl nodded slowly. "The mouse... it went there."

    Jane looked at Isla. The hope in her eyes was almost too much. So much that the crushing blow of defeat would completely and finally ruin them. Isla saw that in her eyes, she understood this could mean everything and cautiously responded, "Well…it could be a tunnel."

    Isla leaned in. "If it is, we dig."

    The girl's heart thumped. "Where would it go?" she asked.

Girl, at My Window

Jane shrugged. "Away. Out. Somewhere that isn't here."

"Is that... allowed?"

"Nothing is allowed," Isla said. "But that doesn't mean we don't try, we have to try," Isla continued, her eyes pleading. "We have to dig a whole, I will sneak out at night once he's brought food, and I will get us help."

The girl had no idea where they would go or what help was, why they needed it or what to expect. She had never had to make decisions, be brave or question her world. It was just them, and him, and the room. Jane seemed nervous, still even sitting back against the wall, almost seemingly peering through the wall on the other side of the room. "I'm scared, what is he finds out?"

"He won't find out, he doesn't care, he doesn't see, he takes what he wants and leaves. His arrogance blinds him, and it has been so long he doesn't even know which one of us he takes out of the room. He points left one day and right the next," proclaimed Isla.

For a moment the air in the room was thick with anger, fear, and anxiety. Jane hesitantly said agreed, understanding that the fate of the women and someday, maybe the fate of the girl, was to remain in that room.

V.F. Gingerelli

To serve him.

Set to expire when their bodies had been used to their full extent like the lifeless fixtures of a home, replaced when they cease to work as designed.

After a moment of thought Jane as a matter of fact said, "Fine but it's just... a hole. A crack. It could lead anywhere... or nowhere, and there are rules." The blind hopefulness of this revelation was all and all short lived. Reality sank in and the expectation of success quickly dissipated; a self-defense mechanism to avoid the letdown of a failure.

"We'll all leave the night after we have finished, so we have all night to run, we'll all dig and only after he's gone for the night. We don't dig when its daytime and, when were done we cover it up."

Isla interrupted, "Cover it up?" What is the point in that and waste away the work we've done?"

Jane replied sarcastically, "well you can't expect to do this in one night, we have no tools, the dirt might as well be as hard as stone. It's almost impossible." She continued, "what's worse is if we get caught. We'll fill it in each morning with loose dirt so its quick and easy to uncover. She'll have to

Girl, at My Window

sit here, she always sits here, he will never know the difference."

With the plan hatched the women began to dig, fingernails grinding against the dirt. Like trapped animals their instinct drove them to endeavor this dangerous task. For hours on end they pound, kicked and scratched their way into the foundation of the wall beneath the floor searching for even the slimmest possibility of escape. It was real now. The hole, the mouse, the discovery—it was all real.

They keep digging.

They stuck to the plan.

They would dig. At night. After He left.

Each morning, they'd cover it back up. Loose dirt. Pat it flat. The girl would sit there during the day. She always sat there anyway. He'd never know.

And so, the secret began.

Night after night, the girl and the women worked. Their fingers tore into the soil, raw and bloody. They fought exhaustion. Dehydration. Their breath came in short gasps. But they *dug*.

V.F. Gingerelli

The women and the girl stood up as light began to peer into the room. They were beginning to feel the connection between the, oh so sparing shimmers of light that flooded the room during day, and the sweet hope of escape they felt digging their way through the dirt at night. They filled the whole quickly with loose dirt, patting the top to camouflage their secret project. Once they finished the women stood up to return to their respective corners of the room but for a moment they stopped and looked at the girl, who had resumed her spot on top of the loose earth.

It was as if, for the first time, they were seeing her—not just as another nameless face in the room, but as someone who had found something important. She didn't know if they were hopeful for themselves or for her, but the weight of their shared fear and longing pressed down on her chest like a strange bond, an invisible thread connecting them all.

As night approached the anticipation built. They had never been so tired, and he would arrive soon. They had little to no water. What they had save they needed to loosen the dirt to make digging easier. When it was finally night, they heard his footsteps approaching the door. What if he knew something was different? What if even without any indications, he could tell, somehow, that they had been up to something, breaking the rules, trying to escape. What would he do, how could he punish them more than this?

Girl, at My Window

Just as it had always been before, a small slot opened in the bottom of the door in slide a tray of food which spilled across the floor. With that, he was gone just as soon as he had come.

Sometime later, they began their project once more, their hearts beat with excitement, anticipation and fear and just as planned the loose dirt was free within a matter of minutes. As their fingers bled, and nails peeled back they had no choice but to ignore the writing pain in their hands. Their bodies cramped from perpetual lack of water but that did not stop them, the rain had soaked the ground that day and it seemed every moment that crisp fresh air poured in they were a moment closer to freedom.

The girl's body ached. But for once, the pain had meaning. It was for something. Every handful of dirt was a step toward something *else*. Something better.

Some nights, the air that drifted through the cracks in the wall smelled different—like rain. Or wind. She would pause then; eyes closed and breathe it in like a lullaby.

This time was different, the smells almost overwhelmed her. The tunnel was still shallow. But it was *real*. Their bodies grew thinner. Weaker. But their spirits—strangely—grew stronger.

V.F. Gingerelli

Because now, they weren't just surviving. They were *hoping*.

She wasn't just a girl.

She was *someone*.

They had hope now.

Girl, at My Window

Not So Fast...

They worked so tirelessly that the day and night blended; all they could imagine was what it would be like to be outside of this room. Outside of this space that felt like their whole world, a place that had sucked the life, hope and light from their bodies. For now, their bodies were heavy, lungs filled with earth. They dug ferociously. Jane, Isla, and the girl had dug until their hands blistered and their bodies ached but today was different. Today, the faint scent of grass and the sound of wind blowing filtered in through the narrow passage. They were close—so close—they could feel it like a pulse of the world beneath their skin.

    Isla cupped her hand and scraped her bloody fingertips through the dirt one last time, and the whole opened up. It was still early in the night could they get

V.F. Gingerelli

through? Could they escape tonight and feel the warm sun on their skin as they ran free, liberated from this damp dark box that they had known as home? A rush of excitement came over them as all three pairs of hands dug the dirt from the whole. Cool air spilled into the room, bringing with it the scent of damp stone and wildflowers.

Their celebration was short-lived.

A large section of stone, where the wall met the foundation had cracked in half, providing a gap but, the remainder of the stone remained intact on either side, certainly too small for them to fit through.

Removing it would be impossible, and in that moment the small hole, a taste of the outside world, of freedom at last, was crushed. The poison of defeat sunk into their bones, their only hope to feel the promise of the world again was gone just as quick as it had come. There was no possible way that this could be the end. The sat for a short time, perplexed by this surprise. For the longest time all the women had dreamed of was to smell the fresh air and feel the wind on their faces. The girl would spend days, months dreaming of what she could do, what she could become. Deep inside, buried by sadness and defeat, she still felt that this place, this feeling was not right, it was not what she was destined to be for the rest of her life.

Girl, at My Window

Silence fell over them as they took in the cruel twist of fate.

The girl turned to Jane and Isla; her face flushed with emotion. "You can't fit," she whispered.

Jane swallowed, brushing hair from the girl's forehead. "No."

The girl turned to Isla and Jane, wide with fear and said, "I'm littler than you."

The women stared at each other, half confused by what the girl meant. If only the girl knew what she had said, what it had meant, the bravery it took. Her ignorance was her strength and although the women would never abuse it, they had no other means to escape, they needed to survive. The girl had to go for help. At least in a way if the girl never came back, than anywhere would be better than here, even if Isla and Jane did not get freedom themselves.

In this moment, the only favor that this prison seemed to provide, was the mere fact that even at the age of five, the girl was so small, that she could fit through this hole. She was so emaciated in fact, that she must have been half the size of a normal child her age. She was the only hope they had. Squeezing through that small hole maybe the only way to gain their freedom.

V.F. Gingerelli

The girl had not concept of "outside" she knew no world other than the one she lived in now but, realized there maybe something else, much more than what was here. And in that moment a flicker of reality or maybe imagination set in.

"But I don't know what's out there. I don't know what to do."

With a level of care and comfort that the girl had never felt before, Isla knelt, taking the girl's hands in her own. "Don't worry, we're going to teach you."

For the rest of the day, the room became a classroom. Jane taught her how to spot safe places: homes with warm lights other people who looked little like her. She even taught her to look for big people who looked like them, like the women and the man, and that when they were safe if they were holding each other's hands and smiling. Holding hands was a foreign concept, and although she was told it was the very best thing, she did not know why how something so simple could be so good. It seemed like such a small thing that held such important meaning.

Isla taught her how to speak clearly and tell their story. The girl's vocabulary could not be more than that of a three-year-old just learning to string words together, and although she did not understand why, she could not make out much of what the women said. She was told to repeat what they were saying and told to change the way she said things for what felt like hours.

"Don't say you were hiding," she advised.

"Say you found us trapped. Say we need help, now. People will listen."

"Most important! You must remember how to get back to this place, to show them where we are."

"Okay," the girl replied.

"Now tell me what you're going to say"

The girl repeated, "Don't say hiding, say trapped. We need help, now."

"And?" Isla remarked nervously.

"Um…" the girl paused, "remember how to get back!"

"Yes, very good." Isla and Jane were proud of the girl. Before they discovered the whole at the base of the wall the women did not have feeling, care or concern for the girl. The mere hopelessness and despair of that space, they all shared together changed them, numbed them to normal emotion. Before now they were fighting to stay alive, remain sane in hopes one day they would get away. Jane and Isla had seen the world, they knew what had been taken from them and were aware of what he was doing, how He was treating them. Until then at least they were at least not dead, but they were beyond repair.

That is how they felt, always, that is, at least until that one day. The day of the girl's discovery, their eyes reopened and relit a flame deep within, which for years now, seemed extinguished.

The air in the room had cooled and night had come. The girl waited in anticipation until finally the women gathered around and unearthed the hole.

"Are you ready?" Isla asked softly.

The girl turned, her face a blend of courage and sorrow. "Will I see you again?"

Jane and Isla grabbed the girl, wrapping their arms around her. The girl stood still, she had never been hugged, never been touched at all. She didn't know, nor ask what it was but she knew somewhere inside that it felt good and warm and safe.

Girl, at My Window

Jane replied to her fiercely. "You will see us again. Bring help. We'll be waiting."

With a final nod, the girl crawled through the gap. Jane and Isla pushed her through and prayed that she would return with help before daybreak. The concrete scraped her shoulders and knees, but she didn't stop. She squirmed and pushed until suddenly, she was forced out on to the long cool grass and into the light of the full moon.

For the first time, she slowly opened her eyes, her back wet from lying on the cool grass beneath her. She stared up at the night sky in wonder of the clear star scape and bright moon. She took a deep breath and felt the cool sweet air fill her lungs. With just one breath she felt strength seep into every inch of her body so much so, that the tips of her fingers all the way down to her toes tingled in excitement. The girl had been lying there now for some time as questions with no answers flooded her mind. Possibilities and adventures endless. As if a whole life's worth of thoughts and imagination came pouring in all at once.

As she stood her bare feet pressed into the cool, unfamiliar softness of grass. It bent gently beneath her, tickling her skin, nothing like the hard, dusty floor she had always known. Her eyes widened, overwhelmed by a night that pulsed with color and light. The sky above her was a vast ocean of blue, stretching farther than her imagination had ever dared to go. She didn't have words for it—this open, endless thing that wrapped around everything. Her mouth parted slightly, as if to ask a question, but no sound came. The only thing she could do was stare.

A breeze danced past her, lifting her tangled hair and brushing against her cheeks like an invisible hand. It carried scents she couldn't name—sweet and green and wild—so different from the sour, heavy air of the room she'd left behind. The wind seemed alive, whispering secrets in a language she didn't understand. She turned slowly in place, watching the leaves of a tree flutter like hundreds of tiny green wings. The tree itself loomed above her, massive and ancient in her eyes, its bark rough like the walls she had touched for years, but this time alive, breathing, real.

The bright allure of the moon blanked her skin like something sacred. Even in just the light of the moon she squinted as she looked up, reaching toward it instinctively, her fingers trembling with wonder. It painted the world in with colors she could not have even imagined.

She stumbled forward and found a small yellow blossom swaying on a thin stem, and crouched down, staring at it as though it were a living jewel. Her breath caught. She didn't know what it was, but it was the most beautiful thing she'd ever seen.

Girl, at My Window

The sound of spring insects fluttered into her ears next—a chorus of whistles and chirps, so different from the silence she had always known. She looked up, trying to find the source, her gaze darting around the ground until she caught sight of a tiny grasshopper hopping along the ground. It was almost a glowing green color in the moonlight. As she tried to grab it, the grasshopper jumped away, she gasped, one hand flying to her mouth. She spun around, trying to find it but it had gone. She felt another feeling, something she couldn't name—longing, maybe, or joy too big for her small heart.

She wandered further, her steps unsure, but pulled forward by everything she saw. A stream trickled nearby. She was told to stay away from water and not to drink it, and although she did not know why, she trusted the women and moved along. In that moment she realized that she had to find help, she couldn't forget the way back to the women, she missed them and wanted to see them again.

She didn't understand what this place was or why it felt so right, only that it was the opposite of everything she'd known. For the first time, she didn't feel small in a bad way. She felt small like a seed must feel, just before it begins to grow. The world was huge, mysterious, and utterly beautiful. Full of potential and ready to spread its branches to see what she could touch. She was part of it now. She stood in the light of the moon, her arms at her sides, and tilted her face to the sky. For the first time in her life, she didn't feel trapped. She felt *free*.

She continued along the narrow path through the forest where it seemed as if a natural line lead toward the safety they had hoped to achieve. She was unaware how long she had spent dreaming as she gazed at the sky or how long she had been walking. Her legs ached with pain. She was unsure if she would have to return with the disappointing news of defeat until just then, the most wonderful combination of sight and smell penetrated her senses.

Girl, at My Window

The Girl at the Window

The girl crept silently between the trees, her bare feet barely stirring the leaves. The cold earth clung to her skin, but she didn't notice. Her senses were elsewhere, drawn forward by something that pulled at her like a thread wrapped tight around her ribs. It was a scent—soft, sweet, impossibly warm. The kind of scent that didn't belong in the world that she knew, the room the only world that she'd ever known on of damp and dirt, darkness and hopelessness. The scent was unlike anything shed ever known and although she didn't know why she knew to follow it.

      She didn't know how long she had walked. The woods thinned around her. Moonlight spilled more freely through the thinning canopy. The scent grew stronger, wrapping around her like the arms of a mother around a child. The scent was a sweetness she could not pinpoint but, as far as she could remember, the only thing that would describe it best was a hug. A warm embrace that she only just learned would be one of the sweetest feelings shed ever known. She carried on and she wasn't afraid.

A soft wind stirred her hair, and she followed it past the last line of trees. There, the path widened and nestled at the edge of the woods like a secret held in gentle hands, stood a house.

The house was unlike anything she'd ever seen. Lights glowed warmly in the windows, and though it was night she saw flowers of every color clustered around the porch and walls, trembling in the breeze. It looked like something from a dream—or maybe the place where dreams were born. She stepped closer, her breath catching as she took in the details: the embrace of light coming from the windows, the faint hum of life and family coming from within and the embrace of that unknown smell which by now had engulfed her senses.

She wandered to the side, drawn toward a window half-shielded by climbing roses. Her feet brushed against the freshly mowed grass. She crept close to the window, hesitated at the edge of the flowerbed and peered inside.

And there she was.

Girl, at My Window

A girl. A girl just like her, even her hair was the same color.

The girl stood in the warm light of a bedroom, brushing her hair before a mirror. The room was soft and inviting, the bed turned down, a stack of books on the nightstand.

The girl wore a nightgown patterned with tiny stars, her hair falling around her shoulders like light. She looked alive, warm, whole. And she was smiling to herself, as if the world inside that little room was enough. The girl did not recognize this routine, she did not recognize any objects in the room or even that it was a room itself. She had only known one world before tonight and most things still confused her.

The pale girl pressed a hand to the glass. Her reflection was barely there—thin, shadowed, more echo than girl, more ghost than human. Her eyes, wide and hollow, studied the inside of the home and the girl inside as if like she might vanish. And then, as she climbed into bed, the two girl's eyes met. The shock of this moment sent trembles down her spine. As she stood outside of the window she froze, as if the warm spring day froze over in an instant. In that moment the girl had forgotten all that she was meant to do.

V.F. Gingerelli

"Don't say hiding, say trapped. We need help, now."

"And…remember how to get back to us!"

She was experiencing so many new things, so many new memories. Her senses overwhelmed by the new experiences she had. A complete overload of emotion.

The girl inside froze for just a second. Deciding whether to be fearful or excited, her face lit with surprise, then something else, recognition. And in that moment, something passed between them. A quiet knowing. She smiled—soft and unsure, but real. The girl outside the window felt something stir in her chest. Something that hadn't moved in a long time.

She smiled back. Or tried to. Her lips twitched, unused to the shape. Just then from inside the home she lifted her hand, just beginning to wave—

But the girl was already gone.

The interaction was foreign. Not only had she never met anyone else, but she had also barely interacted with others before today, never mind one who looked little like her, so similar, so strange.

Girl, at My Window

She turned from the window, disappearing into the dark like smoke in the wind. The scent of the flowers and the sweetness clung to her as she passed through the trees, back into the cold silence of the woods. The night swallowed her quickly, but the light she'd seen—the warmth, the smile—stayed with her, and as she carried that memory, her heartbeat in her chest like a flickering echo that she could not shake.

She moved without thought, the pull that had drawn her to the house now tugging her back, though it felt heavier now. Each step away from that warmth felt like sinking deeper into ice. Her limbs moved slowly. The smell of the home faded, replaced by the familiar scent of earth and dirt. Her world again. The one with no stars. The one with no light, the one with just darkness. As she wandered back the once clear path turned to brush and after a small jaunt through the brush, she was back in the place she'd left earlier that night.

In the rush of experience and excitement to leave earlier that night, she had not noticed the despair she left behind. The home she saw with the girl and sweet flowers looked as if something out of a dream. As she entered back to the hole she had crawled from earlier, the place where she had spent her whole life, she noticed the most rugged brush, overgrown with weeds and ugly things, brown colored misshapen metal objects and what may have been a home, somewhere she had never known, connected to the room where they were kept. She saw no lights, no flowers, no warmth. She smelled no sweetness in the air. This was not home, this was not where she belonged.

As she reached the edge of the wall where she had escaped earlier that night, the mouth of the hole yawned open in the shadows, waiting for her like an old friend. It had no warmth, no scent, no light—but it was hers only because it was all she knew, where Jane and Isla waited for her. She stood at the edge for a moment, glancing once over her shoulder, though she couldn't see the house anymore. She thought just for a moment that she did not have to return except she must if only for Jane and Isla.

Her fingers curled around something in her pocket. A petal, soft and perfect, had come away from the rose bush when she touched it. She didn't remember taking it, but there it was, pressed between her fingertips like a promise.

She climbed down into the hole.

The concrete above caught at her shoulders and hair, the earth tightening around her with each movement. The descent felt longer than before, as if the hole resisted her return. But eventually, the shadows closed above her, and the scent of flowers was gone. The silence returned, wrapping around her shoulders like a shroud. But she no longer felt

Girl, at My Window

alone. Two sets of hands, one on each arm gently pulled her through. Jane and Isla hugged the girl again.

She clutched the petal in her pocket and as if the most prized possession she owned gave it to Isla. A single tear fell from her eye. "Did you get help?"

The girl explained the wonders she saw, and how she had to remember get help, that we're trapped, and remember how to get back. She detailed the extraordinary experiences and things she saw and that there was a girl whose room was nothing like ours.

"I saw so many things; I brought this for you"

Isla felt confused. "Did you remember to get help; did you remember to find someone that can get us out?

The girl felt ashamed. Caught up in her emotion, caught up in the potential of the outside world and experience she had never known, nothing she could have ever imagined.

"I saw someone"

"Saw who?" Isla was confused, half expecting a five-year-old who had spent her life in a damp dirt floor cell to stage a rescue in a foreign world outside those four walls.

V.F. Gingerelli

The girl continued, "I saw a girl, a girl like me and then I don't remember except I was back here."

The morning fog of spring rolled in laying an eerie blanket of mist across the well-manicured lawns of the neighborhood. When morning Emma awoke, she sat cross-legged on her bed, staring outside. Her heartbeat louder than usual, and her thoughts ran like startled birds. She had the strangest dream. What felt like reality, a mysterious connection she could not shake must have, could only have been, the thing of dreams. She remembered a girl just like her, peering in from outside her window. A mere second's exchange and a hesitant smile. As Emma got ready to put on the clothes her mother laid out for her the night before, she turned once more, she noticed the fog had left a handprint in the window where the girl had reached out to her the night before. It was then that Emma knew she had not dreamed this meeting.

She'd seen her. Not just imagined her. The girl was real.

And not scary. Not a ghost, not exactly. Just... sad. Alone. Emma had seen it in her eyes.

Girl, at My Window

She touched the glass where the girl had stood. "Who are you?" she whispered. "Where did you go?"

She found no answers. But Emma didn't feel afraid. Not anymore. She felt… curious. She felt something else…connected. A little ache in her chest, like she'd lost something she didn't know she needed before last night.

V.F. Gingerelli

Just a Dream

All that day Emma couldn't keep the thoughts about the girl at her window out of her mind. She waited in anticipation for the night when she could lay in bed, with eyes locked on the window, half-expecting to see a face staring back at her from the shadows outside.

The memory played in her head like a looping film: the girl's pale face, the way her lips curled into a mischievous smile just before she vanished. It hadn't felt like a dream. The cold on the windowpane, the hum of the cicadas, the soft, eerie whisper of the wind—all of it had felt too real. Too vivid.

Girl, at My Window

Yet when she'd told her parents the morning after, their faces had told her a different story.

"You probably dreamed it, sweetie," Lynn had said gently, brushing a strand of hair behind Emma's ear as they sat at the breakfast table. Her voice was soft, but there was a tightness in her eyes, like she was trying to convince herself as much as Emma.

"But I didn't!" Emma insisted. "She was real. She looked just like me. She even said—"

"Emma," Bryan interrupted, lowering his newspaper with a firm expression, "why would a girl your age be outside in the middle of the night, don't you think her mommy and daddy would want her inside getting ready for bed honey?"

Emma's small hands tightened around her juice glass. "She was real," she said again, voice barely above a whisper.

"She knocked on my window, it's not fake, it's not like a movie, she was there."

Bryan sighed and leaned forward; his brow creased. "Honey, your window's not even low enough for someone to reach easily. And you've been having some very vivid dreams lately. That's all it is."

V.F. Gingerelli

Emma looked down at her cereal, appetite gone. Maybe they were right. Maybe she had imagined it. But if it had been a dream, why did she still remember the exact shape of the girl's eyes, the imprint her hand had left on the window? Dreams didn't feel like this. Dreams didn't follow you into daylight.

Later that evening, as Emma played half-heartedly with her puzzle in the living room, she overheard her parents whispering in the kitchen.

"I just think we need to watch her more closely," Lynn was saying. "She's been acting... strange."

"She's not strange," Bryan said. "She's lonely. We knew this might happen."

Lynn sighed. "You think this is about her wanting a sibling?"

"Don't you?" Bryan's voice dropped lower, but Emma still caught the words. "She's been talking about it more and more. Drawings of two girls. Asking why she doesn't have a sister. And now this? A mysterious girl outside the window who looks just like her?"

Lynn paused. "You think she made it up?"

Girl, at My Window

"I think she wants someone so badly that her mind filled in the blank." Bryan replied.

Emma sat frozen, puzzle piece in hand. Was that really what they thought? That she had made it all up for attention? Just because she sometimes wished she had a sister.

But she hadn't imagined that girl.

That night, Emma didn't sleep right away. She lay awake, staring at the ceiling, listening to the creaks of the house settling. Her parents had tucked her in gently, with reassuring smiles and extra nightlights, but the doubt in their voices echoed louder than their comfort.

What if they were right?

What if her loneliness had conjured something up? She'd always felt it, that little hollow space where a sister might have been. She imagined what it would be like—someone to play with, to whisper secrets to under the covers, to sneak cookies with after dinner. Was that why the girl had seemed so familiar?

Still, something about the encounter didn't sit right. The girl hadn't acted like a sister. She'd seemed…

V.F. Gingerelli

otherworldly. Like she didn't belong. Like she wasn't supposed to be here.

Emma turned to the window again. The glass was dark, reflecting only her own worried face. But in the pit of her stomach, she felt the same cold twist of unease she'd felt when the girl had first appeared.

Maybe her parents were right.

Maybe she had imagined her.

The girl's only thought that long day was that the light that shown through the crack in the ceiling of their room, the light that she once cherished so much would go away. She knew that would be the time that she was able to journey once again. The promise of hope, the possibility of safety for her, Jane and Isla. The possibility of home, and that sweet smell that surrounded her like a hug.

The previous night, when she arrived back to the room, they quickly covered the hole, and the girl sat and waited. She waited for what felt like the longest time. She had experienced something she had never thought possible. Potential. The chance to have more. The chance to be better

Girl, at My Window

than, to have something other than, to imagine more than she had ever before.

Just as night fell the girl felt anxious. "Can we go now?

"No" Isla replied, "He will be here, and we must wait until he's gone, otherwise well you will never see the girl, or the roses, or learn what life really means."

Well, just as every day before the small slot at the bottom of the door opened and for some reason the good thing that he brought on the rusty old tray was no longer as good. In fact, the girl could not imagine eating it. Something about it lacked life. It lacked all color and emotion. She was determined now to return to the house she saw the night before, to a better life, to the girl she has connected with through the window.

He came again and took the woman. He took Jane. For the first time the girl knew their names and for that reason their sadness and somber attitudes made that interaction with him feel even worse. Just as always, Jane returned as quick as she had left. Her demeanor had not changed. That in as much was the same, closed, shut off, without feeling. Just as she had returned the door slammed shut.

V.F. Gingerelli

With out as much as a breath Jane exclaimed, "tonight, you will go to the house, you will beat on the windows and walls, and you will tell them to help! We are trapped, you will remember how to get back here, and you will save us!"

Girl, at My Window

Sky

The earth trembled again beneath their feet, but this time it was with a controlled urgency. Jane and Isla crouched at the base of the wall, their fingers digging into the damp soil. Beside them, the girl stood still, silent, but her eyes burned with determination.

"This is where it was," Jane said, brushing back dirt. "This is the spot, lets dig."

Isla nodded, her breath shallow, and together the three of them clawed through the wet earth. The glow of the moon returned, faint but full of hope, wind pulsed through the opening inviting them to finally be free. The girl stepped forward, crouching low, her pale face illuminated by the light that leaked through the hole. She looked at Jane and Isla, her lips parted as if to say something—but then, she simply nodded. They did not have to talk, they felt more connected than ever, the girl knew what she had to do and how much it meant for their survival, without this there was nothing else. They knew their fate if she did not bring back help.

Isla and Jane helped guide her through the opening as a mother helps a child enter a new world for the first time, frightful yet excited. The space barely fit her small frame. Her fingers gripped the edges of the breach as she slipped through. The girl finally understood enough of this new world, the hope and dreams it conjured in her mind to realize; this was a new life, an evolutionary moment she could not sense the future with all her senses. She had been reborn into a world where she was more than just, "girl." Her silhouette vanished into the shimmering tunnel, and the light pulsed once, then receded into the ground.

The room went silent. Jane and Isla sat quiet, unknowing of the events that lay ahead. Would the girl find the home she saw the night before, would she remember how to return, would she make her way back before daybreak? What would he do, what would happen to them if she didn't return?

On the other side, the world felt different—brighter, louder, like she had been underwater and now burst free for air. The girl stumbled, blinking against the sudden rush of wind and sound. The sky above was impossibly clear; she could once again see the shimmering stars and the crisp

Girl, at My Window

outline of the moon. It was the most incredible thing she had ever seen almost as if there was no end, limitless with possibility.

She turned, orienting herself. The woods behind her looked ordinary—no signs, no life, only the rustle of trees. She knew the way.

She ran.

Inside the house, Emma stirred. The soft light of the moon peered in through her window and lit the corner of her room, casting silver shadows on the wallpaper. She had dozed off with a book still open on her chest. Somewhere in her dreams, she had heard a voice—a faint whisper. But now, there was something real. A tapping.

Her eyes fluttered open.

Another tap. Then a louder knock. From the window.

Emma sat up straight, frightened, the book sliding off her. The room was still. The air felt crisp and clear, she awoke as if she had rested for days.

She turned toward the window.

V.F. Gingerelli

There—pressed against the glass—was a face.

The girl's face.

Emma's breath was caught in her throat. The girl's eyes were wide, frantic. Her pale lips moved rapidly, but no sound reached through the pane. Then the banging began.

Thud. Thud. Thud.

"Help!" the girl mouthed, her fists pounding against the window. "We're trapped! We need help!" Emma scrambled out of bed, stumbling backward. "What—?"

The girl banged harder, opening her fists and slapping her palms against the surface as though trying to phase through it. "Help!" she cried again. "Help us!"

"Mom, mom!" Emma shouted. "Dad!"

She turned and ran to the hallway, heart hammering in her chest. Her bear feet sliding across the floor under her weight as she fled her room.

Moments later, Bryan and Lynn appeared, bleary-eyed and startled.

Girl, at My Window

"Emma?" Lynn asked, her voice tight with worry. "What is it? What's wrong?"

"There's someone outside my window!" Emma cried, pointing down the hall. "A girl! She's banging—she's screaming for help!"

Bryan didn't waste a moment. He moved past them and down the hall, flinging open the door to Emma's room. The others followed close behind.

And then they saw her.

Bryan ran to the front door, unlocked it and called for her from the side of the home. The girl ran over and repeated her chant, "Help us, were trapped, we need help, now!"

She was soaked, dirt-smudged, her hair tangled with leaves—but her eyes were unmistakable. Wide. Green.

Just like Emma's.

Lynn gasped, a hand flying to her mouth. Bryan stepped in front of Emma instinctively.

The girl took another step forward. "Please," she said, her voice hoarse, urgent. "We're trapped. There's no time."

V.F. Gingerelli

Bryan's voice was low, steady. "Who are you?"

The girl looked straight at Emma, her expression one of desperation and pleading. "You know me," she whispered. "You know who I am."

Emma felt her knees weaken. The room seemed to tilt around her. Something deep inside her stirred—a memory not her own, a sense of loss she couldn't explain.

The girl turned toward her. "You saw me there. You saw me before."

Lynn reached for Bryan's arm. "She… where did she come from, what is happening?"

"Emma," Bryan said softly, finishing the thought.

The girl's shoulders trembled as she tried to steady herself. "They're still in there," she said. "Jane. Isla. They need help. We need to go now, they'll be lost."

Silence fell over them. Only the wind whispered. Emma took a slow step forward, past her father. "You came back," she said, barely breathing.

The girl nodded. "Because you're the only one who can help."

Girl, at My Window

Emma, took one step closer, you could barely hear her timid voice, "I'm Emma what…what is your name?

The girl took a moment, she had never been given so much attention, so much choice, what was her name? In that moment she thought everything and nothing all at the same time, she thought of the small tight space that up until yesterday was the only world she knew.

She realized the possibility of her life, the new experiences she held just in those two brief nights and how big and beautiful the world was. So, in that moment she replied not with words but with a gesture toward the most beautiful thing that she had ever seen, something that filled her with so much awe and wonder that she almost had no other choice.

She looked at Emma and pointed upward.

Emma paused and smiled, "Sky, your name is Sky."

The girl flickered a smile and shook her head.

"Yes, I'm Sky."

V.F. Gingerelli

The Beginning

The phone call Bryan made to the police was short, his voice steady despite the tremor in his hands. Lynn stood by him in the kitchen, holding Sky gently by the shoulder as the girl watched everything around her with wide, unblinking eyes. Emma sat cross-legged on the living room rug, her stuffed bear now nestled in her lap, watching Sky with curiosity and concern.

    The warmth of the home, the smell, the same smell that lingered and drew her to out of the woods to Emma's window hung thick in the air. Lynn looked down at Sky and realized, her eyes wide, searching for something anything.

    "What do you need honey, what is it Sky?"

Girl, at My Window

The girl's eyes shot down for a moment looking side to side then...she looked up and in an at an almost imperceptible volume, "what is it?"

"What...?" Lynn could not be more confused by her question.

Sky made a slight movement with her nose, tilting her head up. Bryan had finished his call with the police and the silence in the room was quiet enough Lynn could her the air rush into Sky's nose as she smelled the air.

It took Lynn a moment, she looked around and found Emma watching intently, "Mommy, I know, here!"

Emma ran the kitchen counter, she grabbed the plate and unwrapped what was inside. She put the plate before Sky. Emma watched intently, Sky's eyes opened wide and for a second she seemed frozen in place. They were almost as big as a whole hand and, despite being baked earlier that night they slightly crisp edges and chocolate seemed to smolder. The chocolate chips were little volcanoes of chocolate melting atop the cookie and dripping down the edges. Her senses were overwhelmed. She could not perceive what this was. What to do. Where to go from here.

This was the smell that drew her from the woods, the one that made her feel so safe, the same smell that she somehow felt when she heard Emma and Lynn's gentle voices. Emma took a piece of the cookie and with a small quick glance Sky understood, she too took a cookie and without hesitation devoured the delicious snack.

The cookie filled her whole mouth, it flooded all her senses. Sky thought of nothing in that moment, nothing mattered, the past was forgotten and for that minute, with her whole body she felt the full warmth inside that home. The feeling every child deserves and she never had.

When the patrol car pulled up the driveway the blue lights cast flickers across the walls of the quiet living room, Sky froze. Her fingers clenched Lynn's sweater, knuckles pale. She had never seen the police, the sounds and lights were simultaneously intriguing and terrifying. She wondered if they were there to take her back to the room, to him. How could this safe feeling flee so quick, how could this happen after all she had been through.

"It's okay," Lynn murmured softly, her hand resting over Sky's. "They're just here to help. They're not angry."

Two uniformed officers entered the home—a woman in her forties with kind eyes and a tall man with a notebook already in hand. They introduced themselves as Officer Rodriguez and Officer Carter, and although their presence

Girl, at My Window

was calm, Sky took a step behind Lynn, partially hidden by her sweater.

Bryan gave a quick rundown of how they had found Sky just outside their home. Bryan detailed Emma's strange encounter, their disbelief and the proceeding nights events. He mentioned not knowing, seeing or encountering the girl before now. Bryan, Lynn and the police were bewildered by Sky. What other secrets was she hiding?

The officers nodded, asked a few questions, and then turned to the girl.

"Hi there," Officer Rodriguez said gently, crouching slightly so she was more at Sky's eye level, to see around Lynn, where Sky had been hiding "What's your name?"

Sky hesitated. Her mouth opened and closed once, and then, voice barely above a whisper, she said, almost questioning her own answer… "Sky."

"Hi, Sky," Rodriguez said with a warm smile. "You're safe now. We just want to ask you a few questions. Do you think you can help us?"

Sky looked to Lynn, who gave her a small, encouraging nod. Emma leaned forward, beaming at her.

"You're really brave," Emma said softly. "You can do it."

That seemed to help. Sky took a breath and nodded slowly. She wasn't used to any attention, no one spoke to her and men certainly were not something she knew much of. Sky knew that Bryan was different, he was big, and his hair was short like the man at the room but so many things were different. Bryan made her feel like she was eating a plate full of cookies, safe, warm. His voice was calm and patient, and in a way, she saw those same feelings when Emma looked at her dad. When Lynn and Bryan were there Sky felt as if she could do almost anything.

She was still afraid, but something about the gentle way they were all treating her made her want to try.

As the officers began their questions, Sky did her best to answer. They asked about the women in the room. About where she had come from. What the house had looked like. Whether she remembered any addresses, signs, or anything that might help them find the place.

She shook her head more often than she spoke. "There weren't signs. Just woods. Always woods" Bryan frowned, taking mental notes. Lynn stroked Sky's back gently as the officers exchanged glances.

Girl, at My Window

"We'll start canvassing the forest," Carter said, looking over at Rodriguez. "Get some dogs and a drone up if we can."

Sky flinched. "That place," she whispered. "You'll find it, that's where I lived, it's that way."

That place... She spoke the words like they held weight. Like it wasn't just a space, but a world all its own. A world built of fear. This place she had spent her whole life, day in day out the same. Nothing to hope for, nothing to dream of but a barren space of dirt and darkness. Little did she understand, it was him, that person, his control over them that kept them there. Although the women understood the extent of this betrayal far greater than Sky, she was finally beginning to understand what had been taken from her.

Officer Rodriguez paused.... "That place...the place where you lived?" He softly replied, "What is it, where is it?"

Sky described it, the darkness, the women and him. She told him how they were there for so long that how he came into the room and took the women. She told him about the small sliver of light that peered through the cracked roof and how the mouse came to show her the way here.

Bryan, Lynn and the officer looked at each other with and overwhelming depression and fear. Their faces read disbelief, not because they assumed Sky was untruthful but out of sadness, because they could not imagine finding this horrible place where Sky was forced to live.

"We'll find it," Rodriguez promised her. "But you don't have to go back there. Ever."

Sky said nothing, but a breath she hadn't realized she was holding escaped.

As the officers stepped outside to radio their team, Emma walked over to Sky. Emma did not understand why she was flooded with sympathy for Sky, her face turned down, eyes wide and intent on listening and comforting her new friend. Emma held out her hand to show Sky a cup of hot chocolate. "It's my favorite," she said proudly, holding it out. "Lots of marshmallows. Do you want to try?"

Sky hesitated, staring at the cup like it was a relic from another world. The smell lifted from the glass like fading clouds, it was a deep and rich flavor she had never experienced. The cup was the cleanest and most pure white, and on top the cutest marshmallows in assorted little colors. So many things Sky had never encountered, things so wonderful she couldn't have even dreamed them, so, in a way, this was another world, another universe from where she'd come.

Girl, at My Window

Lynn gave her a soft push forward. "It's safe," she said. "It's warm."

Sky took the cup in both hands and slowly brought it to her lips. The warmth hit her first, a sensation she couldn't remember feeling in her chest. Then came the sweet, rich taste. As she sipped she began to chew the soft sweet marshmallows, these feelings were almost too much. She blinked, stunned.

Emma giggled. "Good, right?"

Sky nodded mutely, eyes wide.

"You can sit with me if you want," Emma offered, patting the rug beside her.

Sky hesitated, then sat. Her legs folded awkwardly toward her chest, uncertain of the gesture but eager to mimic Emma. This was a position Sky new all to-well, a place she had been before but this time, for some reason it was different. Around her, the home glowed with warmth—not just from the fireplace, but from the presence of people who laughed and spoke kindly. She looked at the throw pillows, the photos on the mantle, the bookshelves brimming with stories.

V.F. Gingerelli

She reached out toward one of Emma's toys, then paused, her fingers retreating like she had done something wrong.

"It's okay," Emma said quickly. "You can touch it."

Sky picked it up like it might shatter. "What are these things," she whispered.

Emma seemed confused. "You didn't have toys?"

Sky didn't know how to respond, she had never heard that word, "No," Sky said simply.

Emma tilted her head, processing that. She couldn't quite process that but out of generosity and kindness she proclaimed, "Well now you do, we can share all mine!" Emma was excited to share her things but also sad realizing that Sky's life was so different than hers.

Sky didn't understand sad as something someone could feel, for someone else. She looked confused.

Emma scooted closer. "I am sad you didn't have toys; I wish things had been different for you, I wish you were always here with me."

Girl, at My Window

Sky looked at the toy in her hands, her fingers tracing its edges. "Me too."

Outside, the police returned with backup. Bryan and Lynn stepped aside as the officers coordinated a search through the forest, organizing teams and relaying GPS coordinates from what little Sky could recall. One team set out on foot with flashlights, another prepped to bring in the drone.

As the moon fell the sun began to clear the fog that sat atop the lawns and warm the air. It cast long shadows through the trees where not too long-ago Sky emerged from the woods. Bryan and Lynn stood in the kitchen watching the girls, they had already begun to see how, in an instant their lives had all changed.

Hours passed. The police had descended on the property like a quiet storm—measured, deliberate, but relentless. Back at the house, Sky was quieter now, but watchful. She stood at the window with her arms crossed, her breath fogging the glass in little bursts.

"I can't believe how much Emma has changed, how bright she seems now," Bryan said, observing her from the kitchen.

Lynn nodded. "And Sky, how much she's been through and she's still perfect."

He followed her gaze. Emma was brushing Sky's hair gently, pulling it into a braid with fingers she had learned from her mother.

"I haven't ever seen this light in Emma's eyes," he murmured.

"She has someone to share her world with now," Lynn replied. "Someone who *needs* her in a way we couldn't ever understand."

The words hung in the air. Bryan stepped beside his wife, placing a hand gently on her back.

"She's been through something terrible," he said, watching Sky with a mix of admiration and sorrow.

"And yet... there's strength in her."

"I think they're healing each other," Lynn whispered.

Bryan and Lynn looked at each other directly in the eyes, they saw each other and for the first in a long time, felt connected in their bodies and minds. Bryan put a hand on her shoulder. "It might not be easy, though. Sky's... been through something awful."

Sky and Emma continued playing and exploring. Emma would answer her questions and show her new things. The light in both of their eyes brightened with every passing minute. They were both changing, helping each other, in ways they weren't even aware.

"I think there is some sort of connection that we can't even fully understand, they just seem so in-tune."

V.F. Gingerelli

An Awakening

The living room buzzed with a strange kind of quiet energy—one only felt when something brand new is beginning. Sunlight spilled across the floor in strips, filtered through white curtains that danced with the morning breeze. Sky sat cross-legged on the carpet, her back straight, her eyes flicking around the room like a bird learning to fly.

Sky had begun asking questions. She pointed to the refrigerator magnets, peeling it from the cool metallic surface. She held it up to the light as though it might reveal a secret.

Emma watched from behind, giggling softly. "That's a magnet. It sticks to the fridge."

Girl, at My Window

Sky examined the cordless phone, the light switch. "What does it do?" she asked, pressing the button and watching the lamp flicker to life.

"It turns the lights on," Emma explained. Sky stared in wonder. "You can... make light?" Emma giggled. "Well, kind of. It's electricity."

Sky stepped closer to the switch, hand hovering near it, reverent. "Electricity," she repeated. "It lives in the wall?"

Emma laughed. "Not *lives*, really. It just... works through wires. My dad explained it once, but I didn't really get it either."

Sky stared at the wall for a long time. Her fingers grazed it as though she expected the electricity to speak back, to introduce itself. The very idea of controlling light seemed like something out of a fairytale.

Sky gently touched the wall, waiting for another of surprise, another mystery to be unveiled, as though electricity might be hiding inside, ready to leap out and grab her.

"And this?" she pointed at a photo on the wall of Emma at a birthday party.

"That's my sixth birthday," she said, puffing her chest a little. "We had a party with balloons, and cake, and music."

"Music?" Sky asked. The word was foreign but inviting.

"Yeah! Come here, I'll show you."

Emma bounded across the room to a small wireless speaker on the counter and tapped at it with excitement. Moments later, a bubbly pop song filled the space. Sky jolted backward as though the sound had come from nowhere—her eyes widened as she spun around, trying to find its source.

"It's not alive?" she asked cautiously.

"No," Emma said, barely containing her laughter. "It's just a song."

Sky stood still, letting the sound wrap around her. She didn't know how to process it. The rhythm crawled into her bones. Her fingers twitched, her toes tapped the carpet almost of their own accord.

Just...music? Sky could feel her body buzzing along with the fun melody of the music, she did not know how to react what to do. Emma danced around the kitchen, laughing. Sky almost unknowingly could not help herself and began to

Girl, at My Window

mimic Emma's movements, dancing around the kitchen. "It's like a cookie!" she said thoughtfully, as if searching for the closest feeling she had known that matched.

Emma burst into laughter. "Yeah! That's actually a good way to put it. Music makes you feel good. Like cookies."

Sky smiled, and Emma grinned back.

Emma continued dancing, spinning in circles, arms flailing with joy. The silliness of it was magnetic. Sky couldn't help but mimic her. Her movements were awkward at first, jagged and uncertain, but she kept going. She twirled, mimicked, and danced, her body remembering something it had never been taught.

The two girls danced like they had known each other for years.

Later, they collapsed onto the couch in a breathless pile. Emma leaned her head against Sky's shoulder, sweaty and flushed.

"I didn't know you could dance," she said.

"I didn't know what dancing was," Sky replied, her voice soft.

V.F. Gingerelli

"Then you're a natural."

Sky gave a little shrug, her smile lingering.

By late morning, a call came through one of the officer's radios.

"We think we found it," the voice crackled. "There's a home alongside an old road, deeper in the forest. Looks like there is an old or structure on the backside of the house, we can see a hole on the backside of the wall. We're calling in back up."

The police quietly observed the home, it sat a quarter mile down a side road at the end of the short rock driveway a small white home was nestled against the forest, The white siding looked as if it had been cleaned and the lawn mowed. From the outside the house appeared normal; a mailbox and a maroon colored, older model truck sat, the dew still collecting on the cold metal surface. The windows were open, and some flowers bloomed among the weeds in the front garden bed. Apart from the cracked and withered stone patio and rickety screen door it was a normal home.

The back half of the home was separated by a chain link fence that was overgrown by vines and brush; bushy unkept trees surrounded the back of the home and pricker bushes were spread sporadically throughout. This level of

Girl, at My Window

neglect was easily explained away, normal people were busy with work and hobbies, it was easy to blame a lack of time for the condition of the less noticeable parts of the home.

"Did they say a hole?" he asked.

"Yes, sir. A breach. Looks fresh."

Lynn entered the room, eyes darting between Bryan and the officer. "Do you think it's the place?"

Emma turned to Sky. The girl was still. Pale. Her eyes glassed over.

"You found it," she said softly.

Rodriguez stepped back in from the porch. "Sky, I think we found where you were staying. We're going to investigate, see if we can find your friends. Okay?" Seeing Sky's demeanor instantly change, Emma rushed over to hug Sky, something she had only ever felt once before.

Sky looked torn between relief and fear. "Be careful. He might be there. He might put you in the room."

V.F. Gingerelli

Emma stood and wrapped her arms around her. "They're going to find them," she said. "They'll bring them back."

Sky nodded, but her eyes stayed locked on some invisible place far away.

"We'll be careful, we won't let anyone get hurt and you don't have to worry no one will be in the room for much longer." Rodriguez promised.

Bryan and Lynn watched as the officers headed out again. Emma held her tighter. "You're not there anymore," she said. "You're here. With me."

Sky held onto that hand tightly, her gaze flicking from the door to the music still playing in the background, to the warmth of the drink in her other hand.

"I don't know what this is," she whispered, voice trembling. "This feeling."

"It's comfort, and happiness" Emma said softly. Sky nodded, the words were new but not unfamiliar anymore. Now that she had Emma, someone like her, someone who made her feel special.

Girl, at My Window

What the Shadows Held

The gravel crunched under the wheels of the unmarked cruiser as the detectives rolled to a slow stop in front of the house — a white, sagging rancher that seemed to sigh beneath the weight of its own silence. It sat behind a cracked rock driveway, a place forgotten by time, flanked by a patchy dry lawn. The white siding had gone gray in the dim overcast light. Above it, a shroud of clouds hung low and heavy, and beyond the house, the dense forest leaned forward as if trying to swallow it whole. A mist clung to the edges of the forest beyond, thick and watchful.

Brush and vines wrapped around the back of the property like a noose. Trees loomed in twisted clusters, their branches interlocking. Vines began to wrap around the sides of the home as if the forest was attempting to swallow it up.

V.F. Gingerelli

The mist around the house didn't move with the wind — it moved on its own, creeping up the rear of the house like it was searching for a way in.

They stepped out, boots hitting the damp ground. The air smelled of old woodsmoke and something faintly metallic. The detective knocked, a firm and practiced rap on the weather-worn storm door. "Police, is any one home?" Moments passed. Then footsteps — slow, deliberate.

He opened the door with the same expression he always wore. Impassive, unreadable. The man who appeared behind it looked like he belonged to the shadows. He was tall, all angles and bones, with a face like a chiseled skull — sunken eyes that never met yours directly and skin that looked like it had forgotten how to smile. He wore a tucked flannel shirt, tucked too neatly into his jeans, the kind of too-careful appearance that made something feel off.

"Good afternoon, sir," Hill said, polite, measured. "We're with the county police. May we speak with you a moment?"

The man nodded slowly, without blinking. "Of course," he said, voice flat. "Anything for those that protect and serve."

Girl, at My Window

The door creaked open further. They stepped into a narrow entry hall with faded wallpaper peeling at the seams. Though light shined in through the windows, the interior was colder than outside. Much of the home looked as if it hadn't moved in ages except the trash, overflowing with paper take out bags, and an old leather armchair in the front room where the seat had sagged from being sat on.

Hill held out a photograph of a girl. "Have you seen this girl? Her name is Sky. She was found about a mile from here in one of the newer neighborhoods. She showed up on someone's doorstep, she said she was trapped with some others."

He stared at the photograph a beat too long. The expression on his face lifeless, unchanged.

"No," he said flatly. "Never seen her before."

The detective stepped forward. "She gave detail of where this house was and what to look for, this is the only home in this area for a few square miles. We have a warrant to search the premises."

A flicker of irritation crossed his face, but he gave a slow nod. "Fine. I've got nothing to hide."

V.F. Gingerelli

The two detectives and young police officer moved cautiously through the house. The main living areas were cramped and sparse: a few wooden kitchen chairs, rusted woodstove, shelves filled with dusty books. Everything was clean, but lifeless. The home seemed to step back 50 years, untouched except for a few choice locations where he spent most of his time.

It was the back door, partially ajar, that caught Alvarez's eye. "What's back there?"

He didn't answer right away. "Just an old garage, storage mostly," he said eventually. "Been stuffed full for years, since daddy passed."

The detectives continued down the hall. As they continued the light in the home seemed to darken. It faded as they moved past a well-kept master bedroom and to a door at the end of the hall. A bare bedroom with a queen-sized mattress lay alone in a room, sheets made but a wrinkled dirty mess.

Alvarez passed through a cramped hallway. The wallpaper here was different — older, more fragile. The door at the end of the hall creaked open easily, but it was another door, in the rear corner of the room, that made him pause.

Girl, at My Window

"What goes on in here?" The detective slowly moved his hand to the side of his body, trembling as he felt his firearm with the tips of his fingers. He had been here before, cases like this, where strange things that don't add up.

He replied casually, "Well sometimes my older boy crashes here when he's upset with his momma, doesn't stay long, crashes and leaves it a wreck."

The detective reached down unable to turn the handle on a door in the corner of the room.

"What's back there?" Alvarez asked, nodding toward the door.

The man's eyes narrowed just slightly. "Just storage. Old stuff from daddy. Haven't been in there in years."

Hill joined him. "Mind if we take a look?"

"It's locked," the man said too quickly. Then, correcting himself, "I mean — sure. I have the keys. Somewhere."

There was a beat of tension as Hill and Alvarez waited. The man shuffled away. When he returned, his hand shook just slightly as he unlocked the door.

V.F. Gingerelli

"Go ahead," he said, stepping back.

Hill opened the door, and immediately a new air hit him. Heavy. Foul. Wrong.

The room beyond the door wasn't part of the house — not truly. It felt excavated, carved out of some previous time, or worse, some other purpose. The floor was packed dirt. The walls were metallic, cold to the touch. One rusty pipe dripped slowly in the corner, the place was earie, the drips only getting louder as the detectives entered. The smell was a blend of mildew, rot, and something older. Something human.

The space was bare but strangely full of emotion. There was a smell in the air the detectives could not put their finger on, a thick feeling of darkness. The finer details were barely discernable, only a small sliver of light shown through a crack where the wall met the roof.

"Doesn't look completely unused," Hill muttered.

Behind them, he appeared suddenly, standing in the doorway. "I told you. It's just storage."

The detective turned. "And this?" He pointed at a large, scuffed mark on the floor. "Looks like something heavy was moved."

Girl, at My Window

The police watched him. "You seem nervous."

"I don't like being accused in my own home," he snapped.

There was silence. The kind of silence that breathes.

"Jesus," Alvarez murmured.

Hill moved forward, flashlight catching something in the far corner — scratches in the dirt. Drag marks. He turned to speak but froze.

The man stood in the doorway, watching them. Unblinking. Silent.

"I told you," he said. "Just storage."

"Old damage," the man replied too quickly. "Before I moved in."

He stepped toward the corner and responded, "Okay…well…". The silence swelled again, too large for the room.

Then a voice broke it.

V.F. Gingerelli

"Wait," said Officer Rodriguez, the youngest of the team. She stood at the doorway, eyes fixed on something in the shadows. She stepped forward, crouched — and slowly pulled something from the ground.

A shirt, covered in dust, almost blended so well with the dirt to be seen.

Crusted with dark, dried blood.

Rodriguez didn't speak. She didn't have to. The room had already answered. The police officer and detectives suddenly felt a rush come over them. A feeling of confinement, a feeling of sadness for those that may have been trapped here.

Hill turned slowly to the man. "Sir," he said, voice low, controlled. "Step back."

"What is that?" the man snapped. "That's not mine. I've never seen that before—"

"You're under arrest," Hill said, drawing cuffs.

The man lashed out. Too fast. Desperate. Hill dodged the first blow, slamming him to the ground. The floor thudded with the weight of it. Rodriguez stepped in to help,

Girl, at My Window

securing his arms as the man screamed incoherent words as his mouth pressed into the dirt.

As they hauled him away, his face twisted. Not in fear. In hatred.

Officers moved quickly now. Every room was swept. A hoarded garage in the back of the home, sealed off by years of clutter and dust, yielded the final horror.

Two women, barely conscious, curled together under a tarp and crates.

Jane. Isla.

The air was thick with the stench of old sweat, dirt, decay. Their arms were bound with tape. One eye blinked open as light struck her face. Her lips trembled underneath the gag in her mouth.

The officer who found them shouted, "We need medics! NOW!"

Hill dropped to his knees beside them. "It's okay," he whispered. "You're safe. We've got you. We're here."

Tears streamed silently down Isla's cheeks. Jane tried to speak, but her throat gave no sound.

V.F. Gingerelli

Blankets were thrown over them as medics assessed their condition. Water, warmth, and reassurance from the police officers were enough to keep them alive for now. The women shook with the realization of their rescue.

Outside, the man — silent again — sat in the back of the cruiser, eyes fixed forward. Not a word. Not a flicker of remorse. Only the ticking of the engine and the distant sound of sirens.

Later, back at the station, Hill made the call.

Bryan Carrick answered on the second ring.

"We found them," Hill said.

There was silence on the other end — not disbelief, not joy. Just silence. The kind of silence that holds back the shock or relief.

"They're alive," Hill continued. "Weak. Hurt. But alive."

A sound — a sob? — echoed from Lynn in the background. A gasp. A cry that shattered the air.

Girl, at My Window

"Are you sure?" Bryan asked, his voice trembling. "Are you sure it's them, was this the place that they held Sky?"

"Yes," Hill said gently. "Jane and Isla. They're in care now. It looks like Sky was right, this is where she was, and she saved these two women."

The police continued to monitor the scene, searching every inch of the isolated home that lay in the woods. Sometime later Sky was brought back to the scene. Bryan, Lynn and a social worker were hesitant to allow her to return but, for it was worth, Sky seem unwavering, unbothered by that horrific place that she had been held. She was brave enough to show them how she and the women escaped and detailed their lives in that prison. She had nothing to say about him, really nothing to say about the women for that matter except that she knew without doubt that the women in the house were Jane and Isla, and they were kept in that room.

Sky new nothing of the home, or the man that kept them, no reason for her to be the one trapped there. She just knew that they were and until recently she would have never known anything was wrong. She knew better now. Sky could smell the new adventure, new life she had now, with her whole body.

V.F. Gingerelli

Homecoming

At the hospital, Emma and Sky waited in the hallway with Lynn as Bryan pushed through the door to the recovery room. Jane and Isla lay in beds side-by-side, tubes in their arms, faces sunken but peacefully resting. An officer stood outside the door, reminding them of their safety.

Isla lay in the bed beside Jane as her, eyes fluttered in sleep and, chest rose rhythmically.

Emma gripped Sky's hand. "That's them, right?"

Lynn slightly behind Bryan, hand in hand with Emma and Sky. For a moment they did not speak, it almost seemed as if they were barely breathing. Both girls had never seen anything like this. Emma had never seen two people in such a

Girl, at My Window

bad condition, so helpless. Sky had never experienced such care, so clean and fresh smelling. There were people all over, giving them the most exquisite food, taking care of them, in and out, it seemed the stream of people looking after the women never ended.

After they took it all in Sky nodded. "That's them."

A nurse emerged. "They'll need time," she said softly. "But they're safe now."

For a long time, no one spoke.

Bryan relayed a message to Lynn and the girls who were now outside the room, "the doctor said they'd need time. Therapy. Patience."

"But they are alive."

"And that man — whatever he was — was going to be in a prison of his own, for a very, very long time."

Sky looked up at Lynn and Bryan, her eyes glancing toward the hospital room. "C…Can I..?" she stuttered. Bryan and Lynn look at her and nodded in approval.

Sky slipped into the room and gently grabbed Jane by the hand. Jane slightly opened her eyes then shut them she was letter her know with the last bit of energy that she knew it was Sky sitting next to her, then softly Sky whispered, "No one will be in that place anymore."

"I did it, I ran and got help, I told they we were trapped and remembered how to get back. I helped us, right?"

Jane's hand grasped and tightened around Sky's. She knew she had done a good thing, she knew they were safe now.

The sun was setting when they left the hospital, painting the sky in long streaks of amber and rose. The world outside moved on as if nothing had happened, as if no one had ever been lost in the dark. But inside the SUV, silence enveloped them. The kind that settles not from discomfort, but from reverence.

Sky sat in the back seat between Lynn and Emma. Bryan drove, his hands steady but his eyes often flickering toward the rearview mirror to check on them. The road stretched long and empty before them, the wheels humming a soft rhythm beneath their feet.

Girl, at My Window

"Is that what the colors always look like," Sky whispered inquisitively and suddenly, almost to herself.

Emma turned to her. "Yes, and you're named after it. So pretty."

Sky nodded slowly. "Yeah. I guess so."

They passed rows of pine trees and distant fields. The world felt wider than it had before — like it had stretched out just for them. For the first time, Sky wasn't surrounded by walls. She took in everything around her, there was so much it almost overwhelmed her.

When they pulled into the driveway, their home felt like a different place — not because it had changed, but because Sky now knew what the alternative looked like. Warm light poured from the windows. A blue bicycle sat toppled in the grass. A flowerpot overflowed near the porch. It was imperfect, a little chaotic — but safe.

The moment they walked through the door, Lynn knelt and helped Sky remove the used pair of Emma's shoes she had borrowed.

"You don't have to," Sky said, startled.

V.F. Gingerelli

Lynn smiled. "I know. But sometimes... it's nice to come home and be taken care of."

Sky didn't know what to say. No one had ever said *home* in the same sentence as *her* before.

A few hours later, after warm showers and soft pajamas, a social worker arrived. Her name was Margaret — a kind woman with a file tucked under one arm and kindness tucked into the corners of her eyes. She sat in the living room, across from Bryan and Lynn, while Emma and Sky lingered at the staircase, eavesdropping in unspoken agreement. The two were together now as if they were always meant to be, inseparable.

Margaret cleared her throat gently. "Sky has no known family," she said, reading from the file. "There are no next-of-kin who've come forward. And based on the investigation and her own statements, it seems she was living in that house for... an extended period of time, possibly under illegal guardianship."

Lynn inhaled sharply.

Margaret continued. "Given the circumstances, Child Protective Services has granted emergency temporary custody to you, Bryan and Lynn Carrick. You've already demonstrated commitment to her safety and well-being, if you are willing to

Girl, at My Window

accept the documents are here, just until we can place her in a safe home."

Emma whispered under her breath, "They better, they better, please."

Bryan leaned forward, his voice steady. "What happens after the temporary period?"

Margaret paused. "That depends. Sky will need therapy, of course. There will be assessments. But ultimately, foster care and if there's desire and willingness, a permanent adoption by willing parents can be pursued."

Lynn didn't wait. "We want to adopt her."

Margaret blinked. "That's... wonderful. You're sure? Of course well need to take this step by step and fulfill procedural requirements but that is wonderful to hear!"

"We're sure," Bryan said. "She's already part of our family."

Sky's breath caught in her chest. Emma turned to look at her.

"Did you hear that?" Emma said, barely containing her grin. "You're going to be my sister."

V.F. Gingerelli

Both girls faces turned red with excitement. Sky looked like she didn't know whether to cry or laugh. "I've never had one before," she said.

"Well, you do now. And I'm kind of awesome at it, if I do say so myself."

Sky chuckled. "I've never had a family before."

Emma's smile faded into something softer. She reached out and took Sky's hand. "Then we're your first, and you are officially my little sister!"

They sat together like that for a long while — two girls from different worlds, now tethered by something stronger than blood. The kind of bond that grows in the quiet aftermath of storms.

In the days that followed, Sky moved cautiously through the rhythms of normal life. She didn't quite know how to settle in, but she also didn't resist. She learned how to work the toaster, which lights flickered, which floorboard creaked when you stepped on it at night. She learned that Lynn hummed when she cooked, and Bryan cracked corny jokes when he was nervous. She learned that Emma was messy, loud, and fiercely protective — and that she always waited for Sky before watching anything on TV.

Girl, at My Window

Every night before bed, Emma asked, "Are you good?"

And every night, Sky said, "I think so."

They were perfect, meant for each other. Sky was the sister, the adventure partners that Emma never had, and Emma protected her, made her feel safe. At night Sky would be cold or have scary dreams, and every time Emma grabbed her and cuddled her warm in bed, so that they could both get a good night sleep.

One evening, a week after the hospital, Emma brought out an old shoebox full of bracelets and ribbons.

"I was saving this," she said, "for someone, something special."

Sky looked inside — a tangle of thread, beads, tiny charms shaped like stars and keys and moons. "What is all this?"

"My magic collection. Each one means something. Want to make one together?"

Sky nodded. She wasn't much for words, but her eyes said enough.

V.F. Gingerelli

They sat cross-legged on the floor, stringing colors together, the way sisters do when the world is quiet. Emma tied a purple bead to a cord. "This one's for bravery."

Sky added a silver star. "This one's for hope."

Emma smiled. "Perfect."

They didn't talk much after that — just the sound of thread pulling and beads clicking together, small noises that made the house feel even more like a home.

When it was done, Sky tied the bracelet around her wrist. "I'll never take it off."

Emma tapped hers. "Same. Sister pact."

On a rainy afternoon two weeks later, Margaret returned to check in. She brought paperwork, of course, but also a small gift bag — inside was a hardcover journal with pressed lavender on the cover.

"For writing. Or drawing. Or... whatever you need," she said.

Sky ran her fingers over the cover. "Thank you."

Girl, at My Window

Margaret sat at the kitchen table with Lynn and Bryan while Sky lingered nearby, pretending not to listen.

"Her sleep patterns are improving," Lynn noted. "Still some nightmares. But she's not afraid to come wake us."

"She eats now," Bryan added. "Not fast like she's afraid it'll vanish. She eats like she belongs at the table."

Margaret's face softened. "That's the best sign."

Later, as Margaret packed her things, she paused and crouched down in front of Sky.

"I know this isn't easy," she said gently. "And healing doesn't happen all at once. But I want you to know something — the way you're living now? This is what you deserve. Not just for a little while. For always."

Sky nodded, quiet.

"And you're not alone anymore," Margaret said.

"I know," Sky said. "I have... people."

She didn't say *family*. Not yet. But it was there — on the tip of her tongue, waiting.

V.F. Gingerelli

That night, Sky had her worst nightmare yet.

She woke up gasping, drenched in sweat, her pillow damp. The room felt too dark, the corners too deep. For a second, she was back there — back in the cold place with the metal walls and the sound of dripping.

Then the door creaked open.

Emma stood there in her dinosaur pajamas, holding a flashlight.

"I heard you," she said softly. "Scoot over."

Sky didn't argue.

Emma climbed into the bed beside her and pulled the covers up. She handed Sky the flashlight like a sword. "If anything comes, we fight it together."

Sky turned to her. "I never thought it could be like this, to have someone to help you and be nice to you, to keep you warm and make you feel safe."

Emma shrugged. "You're my sister. That's what we do, this is what we will always do."

Sky's throat tightened. "I'm scared sometimes."

Girl, at My Window

"Me too. But it gets better. Together, forever, for always."

Sky blinked hard. She didn't cry — not quite — but something in her eased, like a knot untangling.

They fell asleep like that, shoulder to shoulder, the flashlight between them just a small sliver of light, enough to remind them that even in the darkness, together, there was light, love and happiness.

On the day of the court hearing for guardianship, Sky wore a navy-blue dress that Emma helped her pick out. Bryan and Lynn sat beside her at the long wooden table. The courtroom was small, quiet. A gavel rested beside the judge's papers, unused but commanding.

The judge asked questions. Formal ones. Measured ones.

Sky answered each in her soft, steady voice. When asked if she wanted Bryan and Lynn to be her legal guardians, she didn't hesitate.

"Yes," she said. "They saved me. They made me safe. And I love them."

V.F. Gingerelli

Lynn's eyes filled with tears. Bryan reached for her hand.

"And the court will consider this a request for permanent adoption?" the judge asked.

Sky looked up at the judge. "I don't have anyone else. But I don't need anyone else. I have them."

The gavel finally dropped — not in harshness, but in finality. A sound of new beginnings.

Bryan and Lynn pulled her into a hug. Sky stood in the center of them, small and fierce and whole.

That evening, the Carrick home buzzed with quiet celebration. Nothing fancy — just pizza, soda, and laughter echoing off the walls. A banner Emma had made from scrap paper read: *Welcome Home Forever, Sky!*

Sky stood in front of it, uncertain.

Emma nudged her. "Say something."

Sky swallowed. "I don't know how to thank you."

"You already have," Lynn said, hugging her tight.

Girl, at My Window

Bryan raised a soda can. "To family. Found, not forced. Chosen."

They clinked their cans and glasses, the fizzy pop of soda and the warmth of joy mingling.

Sky looked at them all — Emma with pizza sauce on her chin, Lynn laughing so hard she teared up, Bryan trying to herd everyone into a group photo — and for the first time in her life, she felt full.

Not just with food.

With love.

With light.

With home.

Made in the USA
Middletown, DE
03 July 2025